W9-AVY-449

Seán Virgo

waking in eden

Exile Editions

TORONTO

1990

WAKING IN EDEN

Copyright © Seán Virgo 1990

Copyright © Exile Editions Ltd., 1990

This edition is published by Exile Editions Ltd.,
69 Sullivan Street, Toronto, Ontario, Canada
M5T 1C2

Sales Distribution
General Publishing Co. Ltd.
30 Lesmill Road, Don Mills, Ontario M3B 2T6

Typeset in PALATINO *by* CAPS & LOWER CASE
Designed by LOU LUCIANI
Printed by UNIVERSITY OF TORONTO PRESS
Front cover photograph GAUGUIN PORCELAIN *by* JANE BANNON
Photograph of SEÁN VIRGO *by* JOHN REEVES

ISBN 0-920428-66-5

The publisher wishes to acknowledge the assistance towards
publication of the Canada Council and the
Ontario Arts Council.

Contents

for Choson and the other ravished estates

and to the memories of

SUNNY *and* EILEEN VIRGO

Q.   "Which came first, the chicken or the egg?"

A.   1.   A reptile laid a chicken's egg.
        2.   The Chicken contains the egg.
        3.   The Egg contained the chicken.
        4.   The chicken.
        5.   None of the above.

If 5, suggest alternative answer _____

_____   _____

WAKING IN EDEN

The Prisoner

The prisoner is led with two others through the forest. They go quickly in single file on the heels of the first militiaman. The prisoner's hands are tied in front of him. Nobody speaks, but one of the guards behind is whistling a radio tune. It all seems very casual.

There are hoofprints in the path, on loamy patches among the pine-needles. Brambles arch into the light and catch at their clothes. There are white flowers still, most of the berries are hard and red but there are black, luscious fruit on the higher stems.

A guard calls a halt, and they stop to relieve themselves. The prisoners are allowed to pick what fruit they can with their bound hands.

The militiamen smoke, and joke with each other. The prisoner stands in a patch of sunlight, smelling the cigarette smoke and the breath of the pines. Wood doves are calling, there is purple juice on his fingers, he has not been out in the air for perhaps two years. The blackberries taste unbelievably sweet and healing.

They move on again. The path comes out of the forest and turns along the edge of a ravine. They can see for miles. Hamlets, pasturelands on the hillsides, wooded gullies. And they can smell the ocean.

A uniformed rider comes trotting towards them. He stops to speak to the first militiaman, leaning over his horse's neck and casting his eye at the prisoners. Then he spurs the horse on again, up the narrow path.

The prisoner steps aside. He sees the shaven jaw of the rider, and the gelding's staring eyes. There is the moist animal's breath, and the scent of saddle-soap and varnish, and then his feet slip away from him and he is falling, clutching at branches and grass-tufts and crumbling shale.

He finds himself on a sloping ledge. A sapling grows from the rocks beside him, straining upwards. He braces his knee against it as he starts to slip again.

Two of the guards are staring down from the path. He cannot tell if they see him. They have unslung their carbines and now they loose bursts of fire down the ravine side. Shales break away and fall around him, a bullet whines out into the air. The prisoner pulls himself closer to the rocks, and feels the ledge collapse beneath him as the sapling tears loose.

He is falling again, clawing with his tied hands as the guns chatter and the brittle rocks crumble. He clings so fiercely that his face is scraping against stone and grass roots. He bites at whatever he can.

The firing stops. He slithers a little way further, and falls. He lies among thorn bushes. He hugs himself to the earth.

When he dares move again his hands are clenched, and stiff with dried blood. He can open only one eye – his face is caked and clotted. He crawls out through the thorns, across to a clump of trees, and falls asleep as the first stars come out.

When he wakes, his hands have come free of their bindings. He follows the sounds of water and bathes his hands and face in the stream. The water runs black and then pink. It is agony, and then the mosquitoes and flies come to drive him mad.

He smears his wounds over with mud. He moves downstream, where the water slows beneath willow trees. Watercress grows in the gravel here. He eats and eats. The peppery, metallic stems purge his bowels; he feels that his body is gorging, all the same, on some essence he's been starved of.

Time is the sound of water and the merciless drone of the flies that hang over him. He eats cress with fanatical greed. He keeps his face plastered with mud. His hands have begun to heal, but he looks at his tiny world through weeping eye-slits. He is less than a man, but it's easy to be so. Time comes and goes, or it stays. It scarcely matters.

He stares with longing at the trout in the dappled shallows.

He gorges on watercress. Tugs a few roots, a few berries.

He tries to remember what he used to be. He has a name, but it sounds unreal when he mouths it. There are images: a woman's face, a fruit tree beyond a gate, the sound of a child crying, but his mind lacks the energy to hold each image down and connect it to the others. There is no full picture. He is half awake, too lazy to hang onto his dream. The only past he is sure of is as a prisoner.

The man who came every morning to torture him used to say "Listen. You ought to understand. In another situation we would be friends." The torturer seemed fond of him. The pain and its smell, the cryings out, seemed only one part of the time they shared. They had long forgotten what secrets he was meant to reveal.

Sleeping and waking are the same state. He has known nothing but pain for two years. Last night and tomorrow are no different.

Then a child comes into this world. A young boy with a thread tied to his thumb, and on that thread a hook and a pearly button. He throws his line out across the pool and draws it towards him. As it reaches the deeper water, a fish strikes. The boy pulls it in, twists the hook from its lips, and drops it behind him. He throws out the line again. After two more casts he has another trout.

The prisoner moans, and blunders out on the bank, pointing to the fish. The boy runs away. The prisoner scrambles on his knees to the first fish. Its tail lashes in his hands. He drops it, recovers it, bites into it. Its flesh is cold, sweet, salty. He swallows it without chewing. It comes up almost at once. He bends to the ground and eats his own vomit.

He waits for them to come for him.

The boy returns with a woman. She is barefoot, and pregnant. The prisoner looks up at her eyes; she stands over him with her arms crossed above her belly. She speaks to the boy, who runs off and returns soon after with a cloth, a bottle, a pottery bowl.

She fills the bowl in the stream, and pours liquid from the bottle into it. She kneels by the prisoner and starts to wash his face with the wet cloth. Her hands are not kind, but they are not cruel either. She rinses the mud free. She tries to wash the scabs from his face. The flies seem to draw back from them. She smells of bread, and fish.

His face stings, his eyes burn. She empties the bowl and helps him to his feet. She leads him into the shallows and eases his shirt open, undoes his belt. The boy comes and supports the prisoner as he steps out of his trousers.

He stands naked in front of the woman. She walks around him, up to her calves in the water, washing his body. Her fingers touch and linger upon the other scars: the burns on his chest, his belly, his buttocks. His legs begin to tremble. He weeps. Little fish peck at his feet.

They bring him back out of the water and help him into his clothes. The woman puts his arm across her shoulders, and holds onto his waist. They move off slowly. The path winds out through the trees, and there is a village.

He tells her he is a prisoner, that he will bring them trouble. His voice seems not to belong to him. "No one will look for you here" she says.

He finds himself walking among people. They watch from their house doors as the woman supports him and his head lolls back in the blinding light.

He is clothed and fed. He sleeps in their house until tomorrow becomes another thing from today, until dream and waking draw apart, until one day the last scab has fallen from his face and the woman brings him a mirror, a bar of soap, a razor.

He does not remember the face in the glass.

Each day he goes out with the men and the boys to the fields. He learns to hoe between rows of corn and beans and squash. To swing a machete and tie up the bundles of brushwood from the forest.

He has a plank bed in a lean-to behind the house. His mattress is stuffed with corn husks that whisper whenever he moves. The lean-to is smaller than his prison cell, but it has no door, and the night breeze from the sea comes in through the walls and touches his face.

A child is born in the house. The corn ripens. One day the woman and her brother hitch up their mule cart. They are going to the town by the sea to meet her husband. They tell the prisoner to come with them.

He has not seen the ocean for years. He sits at the back of the cart with the boy and the baby. The woman holds the reins.

They wait by the town hall. When the train comes winding in along the coast, the boy runs to meet it and then races it back to the platform, waving up at the windows.

The woman's husband climbs down. He carries a suitcase and a sack full of gifts. He hugs the boy and the woman. He throws the baby up into the air and catches him. He laughs. He turns to meet the prisoner.

He takes his hand. He smiles.

The prisoner hangs his head. The husband claps him on the shoulder.

They walk through the square. The woman says that the prisoner is staying with them, helping to work the fields. Her husband laughs and says "Good. We are friends already."

He gives his wife money, and she takes the boy over to the market. "I am home for three weeks" he says. "Tonight the whole village will eat with us."

Has the prisoner's face really changed? "Don't trick me, I beg you" he says. "Don't play with me." He speaks his name.

Everyone on the street seems to know the husband. He takes the prisoner's arm and leads him to a taverna. "You must understand" he confides "The person you are speaking of was shot, trying to escape."

The patrone greets them with shouts and laughter. He brings a bottle and two glasses to the table by the window. "It's a strange world, this" says the husband, carefully pouring their drinks. "Nothing is ever the same." He raises his glass. His smile is searching and wise. "I am glad to see you well" he says. The prisoner remembers the smokey fumes, the bite under the tongue. He stares into the golden liquor.

The husband waves to someone at the door and touches his glass to the prisoner's. "If the world changed, I would change my name" he says. "What is a name? It is even less than a face."

He leans back in his chair and stretches, gesturing out through the window. "I love this place" he says. "Here I was born, and here I shall be buried."

The prisoner looks out, through their reflections, at the bay. Below the pier, the crows and gulls wander peacefully, picking through the offal at the tideline.

"Perhaps" he thinks "I shall always be his prisoner."

The Mute

The Mute smelled fog creeping into the town. By nightfall it would have flooded the crooked streets and turned the warehouses into islands. The lights in the town square would tremble and expand, like lonely flowers.

The fog would be there in the morning, simmering, spreading its loneliness everywhere. The autumn sun was too weak to dispel it; it would stifle the town all day till the shorewind came down through the evening and swept out the estuary.

The grains of smoke from the chimney-stacks, the sighing offal and garbage in the lanes, the low farts of cars and fish trucks: in his nostrils and on his palate and through the blind channels of his ears, the fog was enmeshing them all. It felt strange, and dangerous.

When people came towards you the mist billowed out from them, tasting of clothes and breath and the secret temperaments of skin. But at child level, dog level, a river flowed under the fog. Its essence was wet dust and asphalt, but streaming though it and jostling on its surface was the town's harvest, a kind of soup or sewage which spread through the channels of streets and emporiums to pour at last over the harbor's lip and out upon the sea.

The Mute would run with the silent dogs, breast deep in the secret river. And when he ducked his face through its surface he'd be surfeited by mystery and delight.

He stood at his afternoon post, peering round the edge of the lace curtains. He was always alone here, except when his mother had sewing to do; the front room was used only two or three times a year, it smelled of silver- and furniture-polish, of leather chairs and politeness. When the kitchen clock closed its arms together, lying upon their sides, he slipped away to this room. He stood on the sofa arm and saw himself, slightly distorted, and the room curving round him in the big bevelled mirror. That became more real than the room itself. Then he went to the curtains, and the other glass you could see through.

The sun was behind the chimney of the house across the street, unaware of the fog that was lying in wait for it. The chimney pots opened and closed from the light behind them. When the sun came out again it would be time to move into the hall.

A narrow corridor between the bolted front door and the stairs, dimly lit by a fanlight with two green diamonds of stained glass, and a ruby lozenge between them. The wallpaper felt like cloth and was covered with faded brown roses. On the left hand wall, as the Mute faced the door, was an old engraving of lions in Africa, a male and four lionesses. Wherever you stood in the hall, the lion's eyes followed you.

He only came here when the sun was shining. He stood with his back to the wall, his hands beside him, palms flat on the textured roses. He stared up at the lions and felt the sun reaching down through the fanlight. The air became close, the hall started swarming with dust motes, his arms and his cheeks began tingling.

Slantwise, across the hallstand and the sepia flowers, came the green blur from the fanlight, and at its heart, sharp as a gem, the blood red lozenge. His sun fish.

He knew exactly the path that the light would take, whatever the time of year. He stood and allowed it to swim onto his chest, up the side of his neck, over his face, into his hair. Then he raised his left arm and watched the red sunfish travel slowly along it, till it reached his wrist. Now his arm fell slowly, keeping the sun fish away from the wall or the stairs as it swam through the veil of dust motes. He moved out from the wall with it and waited while it slid from his wrist, into the palm of his hand. He was so slow, so careful. He moved on with it, and passed it into the lion's eye.

Next moment he was running, wrists abuzz, to the stairs, and his cackle of triumph rang through the house. His mother would force a thin smile, and laugh if there were visitors; his sister would curse, and put her hands to her ears, sometimes – if she were alone – scream back unheard. She had begun to think of her brother as a bug.

She was twelve when she discovered him at his game. She could scarcely see him, an outline within the dust-filled rays from the fanlight, but she felt the stale air charged by his concentration, and she watched his hand's shadow, ruffled in emerald green, as it moved beside her and buckled upon the staircase. An unease close to nausea had started within her as the shadow moved on and began to creep over her body. She held her breath. And it wasn't until the sunfish, of which she saw only its thin trail through the dustmotes, was inching over his thumb-mound onto his palm, that he'd noticed her, at the foot of the stairs, her hand on the newel post.

He smiled up at her, his pale face, with its outturned ears, crosslit, and opened his hand to show her. She was drawn in. His eyes moved from the sunfish to her face, and back. Her lips parted, she leaned back against the bannister, she could only breathe in. When he slipped the red spot into the lion's eye, and turned with elated face, she'd felt a wash of heat through her spine, and she clapped her hands to her ears and ran from his shout of glory as he chased her, it had seemed, up the stairs.

From then on he added that gesture to his game, hands over his ears, as he shouted and ran. He seemed to mock her. That day, when she reached her room, she had found the first bloodstreak of womanhood upon her thigh. Try as she might, he began to revolt her.

Was he oblivious to the shifts in human masks, to the echoes of tears or dismay in a room, to his sister's distaste, to the sick superstitious looks he evoked in the streets – that, or blind pity – to everything except his mother's unstanchable love for him? His mother humored even his need to turn aside, like a dog, and stand or kneel snuffing gluttonously at the mouth of a lane, or a doorway, or the gate to the fishmonger's yard. Often she would let him slip out after dusk, at the back door, though his sister would cry "You know what he's going to be doing!" and march from the room.

The Mute could see his sister's face at her window, as he knelt in the lane with the neighbor's dog and quested with nose and tongue at the slanderous air, and he thought that she shared his

ecstasy, while she spied on him and fed her disgusted sus-
picions.

When her face contorted around her unheard abuse, he understood nothing – it was her language, like the language of
people coming out of the fishplant, or the vodka-breathed
doctor's: a language of nostrils and eyebrows and teeth, which
he practised endlessly in the mirror of his bedroom.

And so he was chronically cheerful, absorbed, innocent of
boredom. His sister, who was his opposite, believed that he was
in touch with darker things, like the smells and the shameful
traces he lusted for, the things that should not be known, or
should at least be forgotten, and it frightened her all the more
because he was kept so neat, so clean by his mother, and ate and
washed with an almost excessive delicacy.

Her friends began with pity, and curious small experiments,
but soon they'd begin to exclaim at his sweetness, and she knew
that he *was* sweet and bore his affliction with grace, and whenever her friends had left she would try to be warm to him, only
to see his brown eyes, in his merry response to her overtures,
as windows of mockery through an angel's mask.

She competed with him for her friends' attention. She was a
good girl, and wept sometimes for the small cold cruelties
which he seemed not to notice, but it did no good. She went to
her friends' homes now, whenever she could, and hated to stay
in, the few evenings her mother went out. She, who was learning to understand men's bodies, turned away sickened from his
plump white frame, splashing gaily in the tub when she had to
bathe him.

By suppertime the fog had devoured the harbor. His mother
went out for the evening, tugging her winter coat closed around

her. Her figure wavered into the mist at the lane's end, and vanished. His sister was washing the dishes with her friend. He stood by the back door smiling up at them, but his sister ignored him. A dog's whimper came from his throat, though his eyes smiled up trustingly, and his sister with set face said "He just hates it when Mother goes out," and went up to her room. After an hour she bathed him and put him to bed, riding over his begging eyes, his desire to be out.

He sat on his bed by the open window, communing with the fog. The suspended breath of fishes, the pale sorrow-glide of the wind. He rested his chin on the sill, yearning down for things just beyond his reach; he sighed to his friend, the neighbor dog, vague as a fish through the vapor crowding the lane, and sighed after him as he left for adventure. His eyes and his mouth were wide and still. He waited.

All colour had gone from the night. He saw his mother emerge at the garden gate. The awkward pressure of her friend's lips; her hand on his arm, both clutching and pushing away. He slipped under the covers until she was there, bending over him. She kissed his cheek, stroked his brow; there were tears on her lips, a little wine in her breath. He turned over and sighed and smiled, as if in his sleep, and she shut the door softly. His tongue stole out and savored the woman's sorrow.

The fog closed in. The window became opaque, except where a leaf of the cherry tree brushed it: two drops of darkness spilled from the silver of its touch. The pillow began to drink, his hair was tingling.

He dressed himself and went out on the landing, down to the kitchen. The neighbor dog waited by the gate. They hurried off down the lane.

But where was the river of secrets? The fog and the shorewind intermeshed, deadening everything. The black dog from the fishmonger's joined them, the spotted bitch with the fish eyes floundered over the doctor's wall. The Mute could feel his heart in his chest. His blood thumped in his ears. He hunched his shoulders and hurried forward, hands clutched in his jacket pockets. He came out into the main street, where it curved away from the square and ran straight down to the harbor. But the dogs would not follow him. They drew back, their haunches sank, they made off.

It was as though his heart was beating outside him, between the grey walls of the street. There were figures coming towards him, passing beneath the drowned streetlights. The fog did not part for them, it seemed to breathe through them. There was nothing at all for his senses – only his straining eyes.

There were men in sea boots, with pale faces and wide open, dead-ahead eyes. They marched past unseeing, together but alone. His heart marched with them.

Three women came past, side by side, in shabby coats. Each was his mother – one old, one young, one crying out – and they could not see him. Their faces did not alter as they trod to his heartbeat on down the hill.

The street was full of figures, a tide of people with set expressions. Wild, laughing, terrified, numb. They might all have been dolls. His sister, dancing dead-faced with a boy, brushed past him; their legs moved stiffly, their eyes stared straight ahead. And when they had vanished he turned, and there they were coming down towards him again, and behind them a man with his sister's mouth, and then the Mute himself, clutching the man's sleeve, seeing nothing.

Out of every doorway and alley and sidestreet, from each garden gate, the figures appeared, moving to that same rhythm, coming down through the fog and passing him by.

He turned and moved with them, on down to the harbor wharf. Below, on the low tide mudflats, the men in sea boots were dragging their fishboats into the water. Out on the wharf the women all danced, with leaden feet, and moved on above the sea into the fog. The single light at the end of the wharf gleamed on their slow garments. He saw himself out there, and another him, and when he looked over his shoulder there were three of him standing there, staring at him with dead, mocking eyes.

He sat for an hour, his chilled feet dangling from the sea wall, while the phantoms of the dreaming town passed by him. He felt as though he had been turned inside out. The bloodbeat slowed in his ears; he slipped over sideways and fell asleep on the cold stones. He woke up shivering, the fog even closer around him, and the neighbor dog's wet snout pushing at his ear.

The Mute went back up the hill. He clutched the dog's neck-fur, dreading to let him go. He was sure all at once that the gate would be locked and the house closed up, that he'd never get into the house again, or see the lion's eye burn with the ruby sun.

The Merchant

The merchant sat late in his office, staring through his own reflection at the bank highrise opposite, where Filipino and Chilean women went, floor by floor, cleaning the offices.

He walked from the business district and stopped at two bars where the waiters' familiar deference soured on him, and then he stood in a tile-floored tavern, politely deflecting the bartender's overtures and staring into the mirror behind the bar at the young people drinking and talking; bemused by their clothes, the tribal music, their irrelevance to his world.

He did not go back for his car but walked home. Through districts rising and falling in tone, past renovations, demolitions, re-zonings, between old money, new money, no money.

A two hour walk. For the last half hour, he saw not a living soul.

The only light on his street, bar the illuminated doorbells, was his own porchlight.

A decanter and glass waited on a rosewood tray in his study.

He poured a drink and sat in his usual chair. The walk, instead of lifting his spirits and clearing his mind, had left him restless, uneasy.

He flicked through the TV channels with the switch on his chair arm. The talk-shows and re-runs from other time-zones would not come into focus. He left his drink unfinished, went upstairs and changed in the bathroom, and went to bed.

His wife stirred and murmured a question in her sleep. He squeezed her hand, then turned on his side, staring through the gap in the drapes.

He had not been sleeping well. The business he had built up by skilful delegations of power was stagnant, and seemed out of his reach. With no belief in a god or an afterlife, he had taken to whispering the child's bedtime prayer: *And if I die before I wake ...*

Other men at his age were losing their heads over younger women. He knew two or three who had done that. Ashes in their mouths after two years. The sad revenges of their wives.

Some thwarted part of him was robbing his sleep, but he did not know what it was.

He lay, sweating slightly, till birdsong and light came together at the window, and then he slept.

When he woke he could hear the hum of the city, and the sun was high outside. His wife had neglected to wake him. When he sat up she was still in bed beside him.

She was dead, and already cold.

After the funeral his older son said "Dad, remember that loss takes time to absorb. The grieving process is a slow one." His children used language like that, but did it help *their* lives? "Be easy on yourself, Daddy" his daughter told him.

He walked in the back garden, between the rosebeds and the rockery his wife had created. He seemed not to have been there for years – the weeping mulberry tree and the flowering cherry had grown taller than him. Her flowerbeds were never geometrical, there were no ranks of color. And the rockery was home to wild flowers and stones she'd brought down from the cottage.

He wandered in the garden like a stranger. A hermit thrush sang at intervals through the afternoon, from the bamboos behind the pond. His wife's spirit was in the bird, and she loved him more than she ever had in their time together.

He felt guilt, as his children had told him he would. Inside the house he was stricken by the vividness of his wife's disappointments and her endless, he'd thought naïve, cheerfulness. A kind of faith.

He slept in the room that had been their younger son's. Where three or four times in their marriage he had withdrawn, cold and unwilling to bend, and slept alone. The memory was unbearable.

Yet he slept well, with no night-terrors or sweating, without the childhood prayer, and woke very early to the smell of rain drying, and the thrush's sweet, repetitive call.

He called his daughter and asked her to keep an eye on the house; he was going up to the cottage for a few days. She approved, relieved perhaps that he did not ask her to come. He did not call the office. The business would run by itself, and the directors had asked at the funeral that he take some time off.

He drove his wife's car north. Listened to the classical music station her radio was tuned to, till the signal grew faint, and then drove in silence.

He was conscious that he was not thinking about work, not in any detail. As his business had diversified, the commodities had become increasingly abstract. One girl he had hired twelve years ago on a hunch, ran a branch now which dealt exclusively with "futures". Sugar or palm oil, coffee, pulp, nickel – none of it actually passed through their hands. That branch had no warehouses, and it made the most profit.

As he turned from the gravel road down towards their lake, he suddenly yearned for old age.

The shutters were off the cottage, for his wife had been up twice already this year. He was aware again, poignantly, of his strangerhood. After the first few years he had come only infrequently, though each summer he promised himself, and them, that he'd come for a month. Perhaps two weekends in the year he'd drive up, and then he would bring work with him, and fret for the phone and the papers.

Everything here was his wife's making. She and the children had explored and named the different parts of the lake, and had blazed the trails, drawn the big map on the kitchen wall, stocked the small library. And for seven or eight years now she had come up alone, or had a woman friend visit at weekends. Last year she had hosted a women's retreat.

He had not been here for three years.

He slept in the big Danish bed, or on the chaise in the screen porch. The country air was soporific and the northern lights, flaring each night across the lake, tugged at some part of him like a call to hibernation. He played records from his wife's collection, till the batteries ran low. This was the kind of music, he thought, he should have piped through his offices; but then, as he listened to the water on the rocks, he began to wonder if he'd see those offices again.

His larger travel-case stayed in his wife's car, back at the head of the trail. His fishing rod lay in the back seat. When he walked round the lake on his third day, he was conscious he followed paths that she must have made, and as he rested upon a granite outcrop, polished by glacial action and warm from the day's sun, he looked back at the cottage and knew this must be a favourite seat of hers. He heard the hermit thrush call again, from the osiers by the swimming cove. The spirit of his wife had followed him, and sang out of love and consolation.

He dragged the canoe down to the jetty below the cottage, and sat for an hour staring into the water. The flash of a minnow's belly drew his eyes down through the weeds. Slowly he learned to make out the paler stones on the lake bottom, and then the whole submerged landscape. The foam-flecks on the surface, the drifting leaves and the sky's reflection, all became blurred, irrelevant, at last invisible.

He began to learn every part of the property. He ate sparingly from his wife's stockpile of food in the cupboards, and used books from the library and the binoculars he had bought for her years back and which hung by the door where their children's heights and ages were marked off on the jamb, to identify birds and stars he had never noticed before, and to give them names.

After a while his daughter came up to see him. They spent an awkward evening together and he sent her away, assuring her he was alright. When she'd left he swept out the cottage and cleaned the windows, and walked all round the lake, counter-clockwise.

Where the larger stream flowed from the woods he found a

poplar tree felled by beavers. He picked up one of the wood-chips from the grass and chewed it as he watched the unafraid creatures come back and drag segments of branches up to their conical lodge. He remembered the woodcarving set that his wife had bought him, the Christmas they had all spent up here. It was still in a drawer, in the bookcase.

That night he took out the tools and sharpened them on the stone provided, though only one chisel had ever been used, for an hour at most. And he remembered the blocks of hardwood she had bought for him too, as gifts from the children, and he retrieved one, a fine grained maple, his younger son's gift, from the loft of the woodshed.

Wood, of one sort or another, took over his time. He felled dead trees with an axe and swedesaw, working at leisure, more than once towing a trunk back behind the canoe, to be cut into stovelengths on the tressels beside the woodshed. He took a boy's delight in the work, and in the prospect of work each morning; he scouted the woods for suitable timber and planned the route home with it. He fostered a miniature empire – log-ging off hills and valleys, his mind emptied out of everything else. His palms became blond with calluses, his stomach fell away so much that he tied in the waist of his ragged trousers with a length of string. The woodshed began to fill, he had not heard an engine of any sort for three weeks – only, when the wind came from the south, the lagging thunder of jets high above, going down towards Toronto.

For an hour or so every evening, after bathing and shaving by the dock, he worked on the maple block, shearing and gouging patiently at the hard wood, breathing in time to his work. He left his own litter of woodchips around the granite seat, cutting a sort of waist into the block, an hourglass shape, thinking of nothing, as the hermit thrush sang from the osier beds, but the strokes into the heartwood, with no end-shape in mind.

His daughter came up with his older son, anxious, saying he had stayed long enough, appalled by his thinness. He allowed her to cut his hair, and sent them away. He could not bear the thought of them staying the night. When he looked at the file of things his son had brought up from his office, he felt dizzy. He put it, unopened, away in a closet.

The maple block became two separate cones of wood. He worked on them one at a time, every evening at the rock until there was nothing left of them but the chips on the ground, sleek and uniform.

He sang songs from the musicals they had listened to when they first married, carrying all the parts – happy and ridiculous in the sunlight, knowing that no eyes but the wild things' watched him, himself his own mocking audience.

He found a pair of jeans in the back bedroom. They belonged to his younger son and they fitted him now, once he had rolled up the legs. The same day he caught his reflection in the big window, with the lake behind him, and he took all his clothes off and stared at himself, wondering at the changed proportions of his body, at the imperceptible shelf at his navel, and the grey and black hairs below it. He walked on the stones with bare feet. He began to have thoughts about women, though he knew that the image of his wife would swim between him and any woman, that her voice would echo, even in fantasies.

He sharpened and oiled the carving tools one last time before folding them into their leather satchel. He sat on the granite seat with the axe, spitting upon its edge, matching the birdsongs with the measured rasp of his whetstone. A bird swooped over the cottage roof and close by his shoulder; he felt the breath of its wings. It plunged among the osiers and the hermit thrush ended her song. Astonished, he saw the grey hawk pressing its victim down into the dry moss, its wings and legs flex and the thrush's tail flare beneath it. He felt something tighten in his chest, as if he were there, not here. In that moment the complex scent of the lakeshore seemed to breathe into him. Death had a sudden clarity. The hawk glared over its shoulder at him and then flew off across the water, the little thrush clutched in one fist. It settled upon a half-dead pine he'd marked out for his woodshed, above the beaver dam.

The merchant put down his axe and walked to the spot where the hawk had dived. He picked a brown, mottled feather from the moss and twirled it slowly between thumb and finger. It was warm – from the sun or from the bird's life? The mystery and the simplicity overwhelmed him. He went into the cottage and got his wife's field-glasses. The hawk ate slowly, its neck graceful as a snake, plucking the down from its victim's breast, drawing out meat at leisure. The merchant watched until it was done, the glasses twitching from the pulse in his wrists. Curled feathers drifted upon the stream, out to the lake. The hawk flew off to another tree, preened itself and settled to sleep. It out-lasted the merchant's patience. He went back to the cottage ex-hilarated.

That evening a storm came down on the lake, knocking two trees down, close to the cottage. He lay in the screen porch, a child's delicious dream of danger, as though he were out at sea, and when it was done he lay watching and listening to the calm recover his lake, the half-moon on the settling water, the little waves muttering at the rocks, the pale strands of the northern lights whipping the horizon as the clouds broke away.

All around him the woods dripped loudly into the underbrush. His blanket was damp from the rain that had blown into the porch. He leaned up on the chaise and stared until his eyes made an abstraction of the night, and the screen's mesh came into focus. He was mesmerised by the tight grid of the wires, lit vaguely from behind by the moon's diffused light off the water. Their geometry became a maze through which small atomic ciphers zigzagged. Before he had married he had been in the habit of making lists at his night table, of setting things in order for the next day before he would let himself sleep. The simmering fabric behind his eyelids had danced as the screen did now, towards some order, and he would turn on his lamp again, or write in the darkness – reminders, resolves, inspirations.

The nagging question of the grain futures surfaced from an age ago. It was not really his concern, but he'd been uneasy. They had taken them up only because the price was absurdly low. The old motto came back from his college days – *stumbling blocks* and *stepping stones*, yes. And with things turning out as they were in Europe, he could see it suddenly – a whole new enterprise, action, and his younger son, the boy whose jeans he was wearing now, whose mother had indulged him and packed him off to Korea to study pottery, the boy would come back some day, with his flair for languages, yes, and he'd take it over. The merchant could hardly wait for the night to end.

In the morning he dragged the canoe up and hoisted it into the woodshed roof. He scrubbed his hands, locked up the cottage, and drove his wife's car out from the fireweed and brambles that had grown up past its fenders. He stopped for lunch at the hotel in Huntsville, his first glass of wine in a month. The writing in his appointment book was that of a tired old man; the meetings he had missed, the convention, the trade show seemed now the lazy gestures of someone on the verge of replacement. Before driving on he bought a suit, off the rack, from the menswear store; was amused to realise that he filled the cubicle with the odour of woodsmoke and wet wool.

He tuned the radio to a Detroit news station. Every report had a different slant on the future, and few made sense. He could have been Rip Van Winkle.

Twenty miles down the two-lane highway, a Mennonite buggy pulled out from a sideroad. The merchant's view was blocked by the tractor-trailer ahead, and when it swerved wildly he found himself bearing down on the carriage at 70 miles an hour, the driver's face, under her ribboned black bonnet, a mask of stolid alarm, the horse plunging.

He swung his wheel as he braked, and the car turned around on the gravel verge, slid backwards into the ditch and onto its side, and crushed its rear end against a telephone pole.

He climbed out and stood in the sunshine, talking to the woman, patting the trembling horse, while the truck driver pulled out his bags and papers from the car.

The police cruiser drove him on south. "I feel as though it was my fault" he told the driver. "They often do" the policeman said "It takes time for the shock to wear off." He radioed ahead for a rental car, and by dusk the merchant was back in the city.

He checked in at the Four Seasons, ate a leisurely supper over the *Globe & Mail*, and walked the three blocks to his office building. The cleaners were finishing his floor as he left the elevator.

He sat at his desk, writing memos to all his executives, planning the day ahead.

The Brush Wolf

The Brush Wolf ran out with his sister onto a highway which changed at once into a canyon of light and noise. The ground was shaken and shadows swooped down and across them as they dodged in and out, tails down, haunches bunched.

A cattle truck rushed past, its great wall of tires sucking the tarmac with the sound of skin parting from flesh. The Brush Wolf heard his sister's yelp, cut off in the air high behind him, and then, as he bucked away from another raging shadow, he found himself stumbling on gravel, then grass, and he floundered on down a bankside into cat-tails and stagnant water.

His eyes cleared as he broke from the swamp, and he ran fast under cedar trees till his fur dried, his tail stretched back again, and he raced upon his moonshadow, shedding the smell of his fear with the stale breath of the highway.

Soon he was running for running's sake, his heart keeping pace with his limbs, and he paused when he came to a deer trail and marked his presence upon a deadfall. He breathed in the nature of the place and trotted down the trail. Where a stream trickled out from a rockface he stopped, drank, and turned off again. Twenty feet back from the trail he settled beneath some low hazel bushes. His sides stopped heaving, he laid his muzzle upon his tail and stared at the rippling fabric of the woods until sleep replaced it.

Through Fall and Winter he threaded his way between traps, poison, guns and starvation, until luck and skill were inseperable. Swamp rabbits, grouse, a mink – whatever he saw move. When the hunt failed, he slept and dreamed back hunger. He hunted and dreamed, nothing else, till his fur began loosening and he heard the sap crawl and moan under the bark of the maple trees.

Then he went up, through the farmlands of Egremont, along the old wolf-roads which acknowledge the land's contours, but not the changes that men have wrought to its surface.

At the edge of a sugar bush he met a farm dog, a Collie with amber eyes, and they ran side by side, exploring, hardly acknowledging each other except once when they sniffed round the bole of a basswood tree and their noses touched.

A tractor was working the long field all afternoon, and when it turned back through the dusk, the Collie whined and ran out from the trees, and raced after it. The Brush Wolf followed her a little way into the open and dropped on the freshly-turned earth, watching her catch up to the tractor and go in with it through a gate between the high barns.

There was something repellant about the Collie's eyes, her smell and her greedy motions, but the Brush Wolf did not move on. That night he went down and marked three places along the hedgerow. The next day she was there with the tractor, but though she stood watching, inviting him out, she did not come in to the woods.

He went down, after dark, and marked the high wheel of the tractor. He stole along the back of a barn, listening to the animals inside, sniffing at cracks in the boards, but there was no trace of the Collie. Just before dawn he found himself calling to her, to be answered at once by a rage of barking from another dog, up by the house.

In the morning she came in under the trees, and they ran in tandem again. There was something in her that drew him on. They stood for a long time before she ran off again, nosing each other's tails.

He lingered in the sugar bush. Life was so rich here that hunting and play were the same. But the Collie did not reappear.

The Brush Wolf went down to the barns and found a lair in the granary, behind the calf stalls. He joined the host of outlaw dependents in the life of a barn. There were rats there, and half-wild cats, a family of raccoons in the haymow, opossums in the granary, pigeons and sparrows and starlings. They lived on the cattle feed and the refuse, and upon each other. Owls came in by night, weasels by day. The cats stalked pigeons in the rafters, and fell with them into the straw, half borne-up by their victims' wings.

A woman came every morning to feed the calves, and the new lambs in the other barn. In late afternoon a girl came instead. When she was done she would lie with her books in the haypile below the mow-chute. On the third day a boy came after her. They took off their clothes and touched each other and made strange cries.

On a chain in the yard outside was a dog with no tail. A big Rottweiler, with black and tan markings and wet jowels. It had worn a trench by its circling at the chain's end. It yelled in fury when strangers drove up to the house, and when the Brush Wolf slipped out at night and circled the yard. But when it came into the barn one morning, at the woman's heels, it did not perceive the Wolf, though it was staring right into his eyes.

The Collie was on heat, and locked up in the house. The Brush Wolf went up through the yard and called to her. The Rottweiler raged on its chain. After a while, lights went on in the house. The porch shone out, and a floodlight high on the barn's face exposed the whole yard. A man came out, with a gun, and went down through the barns, and when he returned he unleashed the dog. It galloped off into the darkness, where the Brush Wolf led it all over the ploughlands and the man called and called it in vain. When at last it came back, exhausted and mud-drenched, he cursed it and slapped its face with the chain as he tied it up.

When he opened the house door, and turned to switch off the outside lights, the Collie slipped out past his legs.

The Brush Wolf trotted beside her through the yard, his face by her flank, with alert, mincing steps. The Rottweiler strained to get at them, its voice getting shriller as the chain dragged it upon its hind legs. The Collie stopped, and her haunches dipped. The Brush Wolf lifted his front leg over her back, and mounted her. The chain cut deeper into the Rottweiler's neck; he gasped as he lunged and swung. A few feet in front of him the Wolf and the Collie stood patiently, rump to rump, tied by their passion, tongues lolling. Their smell filled the yard. A puppy's howl broke from the guard dog's throat.

A window flew up in the house and the girl's voice shrilled out. A moment later the Brush Wolf pulled free from the Collie, and she followed him down between the barns. The Rottweiler strained like a sled-dog, watching the couple go out through the gate by the sheepfold. They rolled by the fence together, smelling themselves in each other, stretching their front legs flat on the grass and then leaping off in a circular chase, mock growls in their throats. The Rottweiler's raging echoed between the barns and the house.

A group of sheep broke away from the watering-trough, and the Collie crouched, ears down, and sidled towards them. She slipped in and out, by their flanks, turning them back. The Brush Wolf responded: he cut to the centre of the herd and dragged down a small ewe as the sheep panicked around him and filled the night with their cries. The Collie raced through the paddock, darting and nipping, but the whole flock was running now, wherever it might, hurling itself against fences, bunching in corners.

The Collie ran up to the Brush Wolf, and smelled the blood. She whined and licked his face, and then bent to the torn throat of the sheep. The creature's sides were still palpitating, pumping its life onto the grass.

At that moment the Rottweiler's chain gave way – the hasp tore free from the post and the dog came charging between the barns, chain dragging behind it, baying in fury. The lights were back on in the yard, and the man was shouting.

The guard dog leaped into the paddock, its chain rasping across the fence-rail, and the sheep plunged in every direction. It stood, wavering, eyes mad with confusion. The sheep's pandemonium, the lure of the Collie, the blood on the grass; and the Brush Wolf staring, its hackles bristling.

The man was running in the yard, yelling for his dog. The Rottweiler turned for a moment, the Collie slunk off by the barn, the Brush Wolf became a shadow and merged with the night.

He went up by the hedgerow, leaving his mark on a rock by the edge of the sugar bush. He heard the gunshot, and trotted on through the trees to a pool of springwater where he drank, and slept.

Two weeks later he came back through the township, following the wolf road down the valley side. He saw the buzzards floating and dropping in to the scrub round a sand-quarry, and he turned aside to investigate. The sandpit filled up with the breath of their scattering wings. Some flew with scraps dangling from their beaks. They circled above him, and two of them sat on the branch of a dead cedar, peering down with their naked, red faces.

There was rusting machinery and mildewed hay-bales, a pile of old tires. Sandswallows crisscrossed the pit, twittering at the mouths of their burrows. The place was ripe with the smell of dead meat.

The torn and bloated carcass lay by the tires, stretched out like a man. The black and brown skin was peeling out on the damp sand. The Brush Wolf went down and sniffed, but he stayed for a few minutes only, to torment the buzzards.

The Golden Crane

The Golden Crane stared out through the bars of its enclosure, facing southwest, as it did almost every day, poised on its right leg. Small city birds came in at the bars, or through the wire- mesh overhead, to scavenge around the Crane's foot and among the feed-troughs behind it.

Two tree trunks, without bark or limbs, angled across the enclosure, and there was a horizontal perch between them for the Goura Pigeons. The trunks were bleached white, and streaked with droppings, except where they were planted in the ground and a damp stain of algae coated them. The earth in the pen was black, packed hard and lifeless, with depressions here and there, scummed with rotting feathers.

Four Demoiselle Cranes shared the space as well as the big ground pigeons and a variety of pheasants which stalked endlessly around the perimeter. But visitors stopped at the enclosure because the sign told them the Golden Crane was the only one of its kind left in the world.

The Golden Crane ignored the people, even the sudden alarms of small boys. Its grey, orange-rimmed eyes stared out unflinching as they crowded to the bars, read out the words on the sign to each other, and played repeatedly the tinny recorded message on the coin-operated guide.

The Crane had come, as a young adult, from a trader in the Philippines. No one knew where it had been captured, and no one had ever seen or heard of its kind since then. It had been at the zoo for twenty-five years, and in that time the world had been opened up, all possible secret habitats settled or explored.

The voice on the recorder explained these things. It suggested that native hunters might have killed the birds off, or that logging had disturbed their nesting grounds. Other cranes of this size, it said, rarely lived more than thirty years, even in captivity. The bird had been adopted as a symbol by the Zoo's youth membership; posters, tee-shirts and pins were on sale at the gates.

The Golden Crane was fed on fruit, and a mixture of fish-scraps, grain and mealworms. It ate in the morning, as soon as the keeper had left, and then took up its stance near the front of the pen, groomed wings and breast with its sharp black beak, and began the staring vigil.

Each spring since they'd been placed in the enclosure the Demoiselles had paired off and performed their mating dance on the hard earth, and in the last three years they had made straw nests on the cement floor of the shelter. Sometimes their eggs hatched, and then the Golden Crane had eaten the chicks, though none of the keepers knew.

The pheasants stalked around it, and sometimes a sparrow or starling would perch on its back and pick undisturbed through its feathers. In summer the enclosure pulsed with the crood of the Goura Pigeons, parading and mating on the shelter at the back of the pen.

Some years, in late spring, when Antares flared at dawn on the southern horizon, the Crane held out its wings and called – a grating cry, like an oboe filled with seeds, which echoed among the buildings and prompted a brief pandemonium of peacock screams and the sobbing mockery of gibbons from the ape-house.

An expert came from Japan and danced with the Golden Crane. A television crew filmed him as he stood in the south-west corner of the enclosure and began an abrupt, sidelong quadrille, his arms held out and angled in stiff, semaphoric gestures. The wattle beneath the Crane's beak grew pink, with blue veins, as it moved, crying continuously, in time with the shirt-sleeved, elderly man. The Golden Crane was a male, he said, and he wrote about it in a popular magazine.

Its closest relatives, he said, were the Imperial Cranes of Manchuria. He proposed that before the Golden Crane died, its semen be harvested and used for crossbreeding with captive Manchurian birds. If their offspring were fertile, the gene-pool could be preserved. Selective line-breeding might even recover the species.

And then, on an island southwest of Mindanao, some villagers found the Cranes. Burning a jungle clearing to extend their gardens, they had fired a reed bed and flushed half a dozen birds. The Cranes had circled for hours, calling, and a government health official who was in the area had gone into the smouldering swamp-fringe and found one undamaged nest, with two eggs, and a young bird, singed but alive.

The eggs were recovered and hatched. The fledgling survived, though with one wing irreparably damaged. They were indeed Golden Cranes. Nothing more was seen of the adult birds, and the orphans were moved to a private zoo in Hawaii. They turned out to be females, and after three years the music millionaire who owned them shipped them to mainland America. He had gifted them to the zoo where their brother lived, along with a glass pavilion in his name. There was an acre of summer paddock and, indoors, an authentic swamp environment maintained by computer sensors and a staff of five.

At two every afternoon, and at peak visiting hours, a thunderstorm broke out under the glass roof. Lightning streaked along laser-tracks, fans churned the tropical foliage, water fell down in sheets, and the sounds of the storm came quadraphonically blaring. Afterwards, parrots and drongos swooped through the dripping branches, and Philippine butterflies dried their wings, while the young Cranes stepped through the marsh-grasses, picking at seeds, or spearing the frogs and tadpoles which thronged the shallow pools.

Outside, the last snowbanks were rotting beside the roadways. Exotic animals appeared at the doors of their winter quarters. Migrant birds started to drop in, thronging the bare trees overnight and raiding the paddocks before they flew on. The first snow geese cried under the stars, on their way to the Arctic. The Golden Crane was shepherded into a squeeze-cart and taken by night to the darkened pavilion.

Daybreak was heralded by an outcry of junglecocks, and the fading out of the insect sonatas which had played through the night. The air was moist and still; invisible moulds exhaled from the underbrush as a light slanted in through the swamp, far brighter than the grey dawn beyond the glass roof. Small ground birds moved through the quake-grass plot beneath the viewing-platforms, and the larger parrots shook out their wings and glided across to their feed-boxes. A faint breeze, as if from the ocean, began to stir in the trees and with that, the sound level rose – the white noise of a distant waterfall, the harping of bullfrogs, the staccato shrieks of marauding cockatoos. The soundscape continued all day, looping, authentic, overridden from time to time by the thunderstorms.

The Golden Crane stole into a thicket of spear-grass and stayed there, motionless and almost invisible, for two days. The next morning the keepers found it down by the main pool, feeding steadily on tadpoles. By midday the young Cranes were standing across the water, watching it. The video cameras were switched on, the microphones tuned. It saw the three birds' reflections in the pool, looked up, and returned to its feeding.

By the end of a week, the young birds were trailing their brother, feeding as close to him as he would allow. He lunged at them sometimes with his beak, and retreated at night to the spear-grass, but the feathers upon his neck were becoming lustrous and thick, and the wattle was swelling at his throat.

Nobody saw the moment the dance broke out. The pavilion was filled with the blaring of woodwinds and there was a mad, huddled confusion at the heart of the plantain grove. The Golden Crane burst out upon the quake-grass, scattering smaller animals, and its sisters came after it. Their wings were held stiffly out, and they cried from uplifted beaks as they closed in on him with sideward, stamping leaps. He turned and began to dance to their faces, but panicked again as they moved in closer, and ran trumpeting down through the pools, neck pumping, floundering into the bushes.

They pursued him everywhere, crying, dancing, cornered him in his spear-grass den and lashed at him with their beaks when he burst out through them. He hurled himself at the opaque glass walls, and the keepers switched on the thunderstorm. They came in and herded the young birds away, still blaring and dancing, and smothered the Golden Crane in a horse-blanket, and carried him off.

They were taking no chances. Next morning he was taken out round the ring road to the zoo's infirmary. He was weighed, sedated and strapped on his back to an operating table.

His belly was shaved. An incision was made on the right, below his ribs. They retrieved what they could from his reproductive tract, and sewed him up.

The straps were removed from his legs and wingpits. The lights were turned off. An assistant there, a veterinary student, saw the bird's reflection in the glass of the operating lamp. Its wings and neck outstretched, the legs extended. "Look" she said "it's as if he was flying!" They left for a coffee break.

A few moments later a delivery man pushed in through the admittance bay doors. He found the Golden Crane struggling to its feet by the operating table. He stared as it reached its full height, standing above him unsteadily, its head weaving, the bald scar on its belly livid and gleaming. It lurched against the table, then took two steps towards him. He pushed his trolley at it and ran off, calling for help. The Crane made its way towards the light.

Before it were two steps and a ramp, and beyond them bushes, trees and open sky.

It staggered up the steps. A car passed in front of it. The air was cold.

It saw the stars in the midday sky through the glaze of blue sunlight. There were paths and signatures there, vague figures and echoes, with no metal grid between.

Its first, deep wingbeats brushed the cement and rowed through the kerbside shrubbery. Its legs dragged behind it. As it rose, befuddled, towards the treetops across the street, a car braked and swerved and the windshield rapped at its feet. It tumbled onto the pavement, climbed a few feet again into the air, then settled back on the blacktop.

Its legs were folded beneath it, its beak was tipped down on its breast. It might have been a mother bird, brooding on eggs.

The pale, warted membranes crept up upon its eyes. More cars stopped. People stood round at a safe distance. A couple took photographs.

Two men came running up the steps and threw a soft net over the Golden Crane. They carried it back to the infirmary, and tended to it. A few days later it was back in the pen, among the pheasants, the dainty Demoiselles, the crooning, uxorious ground pigeons.

It resumed its familiar post, steady upon one leg, staring southwest through all the afternoons.

The Falcon

The Falcon came down upon a dead branch and looked out towards the sea. It ordered its breast feathers, raked each wing in turn with a hind claw, and fell into a dream.

It sat for five hours, into late afternoon, without moving, except that the eyelids crept up and down a few times each hour, and the nostrils occasionally flared.

A person watching the bird might have guessed (an attempt to unriddle – which is to reduce – the monstrous, tormenting stillness on that branch) that the creature's blood had returned to the flow of the universe. That guess would be partly true.

But the bird is both there and not there. Like a singular child in a brown study.

Its waking nostrils felt a whisper of juniper smoke. Its waking eyes stared unfocussed at the horizon till the sky became its eyelid, and it entered the dream.

It dreamed, as all animals do and as we, at the heart of a reverie, might also dream, of its making. Not the conception of the bird itself, but of its kind. And the makers in that dream are so close to human in their form and movement, that the animals are confused in their dealings with us.

Translucent, transtemporal, the living perpetual walls of *thuja* and *gingko* wood. Never consumed, the knucklebone juniper coals in the braziers. The murmur of voices, soft laughter, the measure of bells. The hesitant, careful footsteps of a certain apprentice.

There's no word in our language which means *"He or She"*. No word for *"He/She"*. And *"It"*, being neutral, is too far removed, for this story, from both Human and Angel.

I brought in a natural thing this morning – an aspen leaf from the beaver-pond – and have let it fall, to decide.

Black/He, Silver/She.

It dips and spins, and is tumbled over by the heat of the woodstove. It lies on the hearth like a black penny. He.

He walked, walks, shall sometime walk with special care.

He dreamed that the form he was carrying out to the drying racks might be the masterpiece.

Dreamed that his part in its making might elevate him.

That even, unthinkably, his Master might step aside ...

Already the surface of the bird was drying, white patches upon the grey clay. He moved carefully, head bent over his burden, hands cradled under the linen shawl on which the creation lay.

He had passed, has passed, shall have passed this way, it seemed, an infinite number of times. Grown not weary, but charged with desire. He believed that he saw things a heartbeat before his Master. He could always predict now what the Master would do. He could, he felt, do it all himself. But there was, is, shall be no end to apprenticeship.

If by a miracle the Master upheld this piece. If it were glazed and fired (with his hand's part in each stage) and then brought from the kiln and approved. If it were given breath and released into Time, would he also be chosen? Be given Masterhood, his own space to be filled in the Fabric, his own atelier?

He crossed the courtyard, where water played and the light danced over the form he carried. Other apprentices heard him crooning to himself. He was sure it was perfect. As nearly perfect as could be allowed.

He longed for change. His footfalls echoed as he passed again into the cloisters' covered walkway. That his potential be realised, that he be given power. An eternity of discipline, patience, obedience. The inflexible system. Dreaming was his only exercise of freedom, and without freedom how could there be creation?

But he loved the work more than himself. He knew that his dreams might tarnish its perfection, and even as he reproved himself he realised that the Master had forgotten – yes, forgotten to mar the piece; had omitted the last, vital, minute stroke of damage (an elbow-nudge, thumb-smear, or nail-stroke), the refusal of perfection that was Life's hallmark.

The inner exultation was so great that his limbs went cold. He turned his face from the others who watched him pass. The Master had faltered. He carried a perfect creature, and only he knew it, and his own ambition was the vital flaw in it. It *would* be chosen.

Trembling, he hurried inside, and at the drying-hall's threshold he tripped, trips, shall forever be tripping, clutching the doorway and swivelling inwards as the precious cargo flew out upon the floor into ruin.

The sound of an egg at the end of its fall from the nest. The aroma of kneaded clay.

He fell on his knees. The apprentices of the place came hurrying over, the hall rippled with their laughter, the laughter that heals by commending inexperience. He was laughing too.

But the bird was cracked open, misshapen, smudged. The intricate mass that packed its interior was split into many fragments. Just one of the eggs rolled away in a wide, unsteady circle, and a new apprentice retrieved it and handed it back, solemn-eyed.

He wrapped it in the linen shawl and left the hall, while they swept up the broken clay. For them, just another small accident.

He stood in an empty corridor, refusing to accept the loss, his failure, the merciful eyes of his Master. The egg was intact. The linen shawl held the imprint of the bird's wing.

He passed through the walls into nothingness and at once began to conjure the landscape: that part of the Fabric – multiform, manifold – which was their province.

Around him, out of a mist, grew a scattering of birch trees. Stones jutted, moss-cloaked, from the sparse earth. Bracken ferns rustled, flies boomed, there was thyme and mint in the air, and a hill-stream rushed through.

Beyond the trees there was open moorland and low cliffs, with heather and lonely thorntrees, quaking cotton-grasses, a wide sky. A hare limped past, a family of chickadees went overhead, fawn-breasted, flying and calling in bouncing flurries. A larksong cascaded high overhead, a raven's cry echoed across the cliffs.

He breathed in the essence of the waiting land. The color, light, perfume – the colors most of all, blended and cherished by the evening sun: wet rocks, a wavering plume of water, late snow-patches on the fells, the haze of whin, heather, stone. And in all this a vacancy: a longed-for cry, energy, talons, a whistle of wings.

He closed his eyes, and passed back through the living walls.

The bells were silent, the atelier dreamed with the Master, and the wheelhouse was empty.

But when the clay was wedged and centred a terrible doubt possessed him. The place was haunted by himself and his Master. He stood empty; self-consciousness chilled the room. The knowledge, he knew, was there in his hands and his heart, but he felt like a novice.

He moved through the room, rehearsing the very first lessons, so long absorbed that they seemed a forgotten language.

The snake foundation, the spinal ridge. The left hand right hand blueprint of symmetry laid down for all animals. The harmonic balances (the high-left heart, the low-right liver). The skin. The seam. Transpiration.

He remembered the yearning moorlands. Imaged his hands as a bird's beak, weaving a nest of heather-stems, bents and sheepswool in the lee of a granite boulder. He heard the whistling cry that would knit the sky's fabric together. Felt the wings in the back of his mind. He bent over the wheel.

When the bells started in again, softly, to the fountain's dance, he was back in the drying-hall, greeting the new apprentices with the bird in his hands.

The Falcon shifted on its branch. A pair of crows swooped round the tree, mocking, but it ignored them. Even when they perched beside it, bobbing and scolding. They saw themselves mirrored in the abstracted eyes and grumbled uneasily, abandoning their sport to drop down the hillside, in long slow glides towards the valley floor.

The Master stood to the right of the table, his assistant to the left. The bird lay between them. On the surface all was symmetry: the apprentice's brush mirrored the Master's exactly. Their shadings blended over the seam. They finished the wings, painting so exactly in unison that the Master laughed in delight. There was singing out in the halls. Sometimes the apprentice seemed almost to anticipate; the Master might have been following his pupil.

The bird came through the fire unflawed. "It is perfect" said the Master "Isn't it?" For a moment his eyes looked teasingly into his pupil's, and then he held up the creation for the gathered apprentices. "It is finished" he said quietly, smiling, and turned to unlock the window on Time.

He held the bird out. It shuddered upon his hand. Its eyes opened and it stared back in for a moment, black brilliant mirrors.

Its tail quivered, and it slipped from the Master's hand, flying fast through the element, its wingtips shaping a tunnel of light. The wingbeats came echoing back like the laughter of children, and filled the atelier.

The Falcon woke, looked out and, in a flickering instant, was gone round the hillside into the hunter's light.

The Master stepped back from the window and held up his hands. And he laughed, laughs, shall always be laughing at the way of it.

The Scream

*T*he scream filled the hollow place in the hillside like a thin, consistent mist which touched everything, pouring and licking into each possible recess. It filled the space between wall and stone, between rock and pool, between tree and beast. It created the space around the two animals that made it.

The boy entering that place and moment in time to absorb it and be absorbed, his mouth not yet closed upon the shout he'd let loose only seconds before when his dog had leaped off ahead, staring now through the leaves of the sparse thorn tree, the old walls curving above him, the sky a shade paler than his thirteen year old eyes.

He caught the instant of savagery at its peak, the hare inverted above the sharp tooth-stones, screaming, its neck breaking in the jaws of the grey dog which had run it down in that maze and seized it and, out of instinct, snapped it above its head to make an end. The fabric of his eyes seemed to tear, rehearsing the charts of his mind for recognition, like the craquelure of an old landscape painting.

A boy who knew more about hares than most people could. Three skeins of knowledge come down through unlettered tenant-farmers. That the hare makes one form to the east of a wall for the morning, and another to the north for the evening; that she'll mate, on the run, while pregnant, and hold one clutch of embryos waiting till she needs them; that the buck hare runs mad when the blackthorn blooms, and goes on two legs.

That a started hare runs thirty paces, then stops and looks back – no sport, but clean killing; and that she runs in a circle and comes round again to the gun, if you smoke and wait.

That a hare must be always called *she*; that to bring her, dead, over a threshold without first plucking her tail for the fairies, her kin, invites sickness into the house.

And if, when this moment passed, he pulled off the tail, with a quick upwards gesture against the body's grain as one kills a chicken or pulls a tooth (as the dog killed the hare) he claimed kin as he did so with the generations of this place who had fostered and bequeathed their superstitions, and with the presences, too, which they fear and honor.

He looked in on the ragged crop of stone teeth, with no archaeologist's knowledge that this was a *cheval-de-frise,* an iron age baffle against men or chariots who might assail the walls above, or that it was much like the tank-trap in which his grandfather had choked upon mustard gas and dissolved, long before his own birth, with his father, even, unborn, into the mud of Passchendaele. He saw the giants' teeth, and his dog's head and shoulders, and the hare whose scream closed on him like driven sleet and ached in the bones of his face. He put his hand out to the red boulder, and caught his breath. His heart floundered on.

The scream was the meeting of two animals and lineages: the wild and the man-made. The grey dog out of the legends of wolves and giants (like these curving walls which are haunted by fairies at night but were raised by giants) surviving through later ages but decayed, as a tea rose reverts to its sweetbriar stock or a christened apple to its hedge-crab forebear. The Hound of Cullin at once lost and preserved in the genes of a rangier, coarser pup from a farm-collie litter, picked out by a member of the foreign ascendancy who, safe after centuries of conquest, dreamed of restoring the warhounds and pomp of the fabled Celtic nobility, long gone under sod and ruin and over the sea or into the genes of the peasantry and who were in truth no more noble than this Englishman's tribe but had honored poets and so won fame and seem to outsiders and readers and dreamers to ghost this whole stony landscape. The Englishman, whose grandchildren would take his family name into the same oblivion and shame of Passchendaele, bred back almost half his life for the great Hound of Cullin, creating a pony-high creature of sweet and turbulent disposition enshrined to this day in studbooks from Melbourne to Pittsburgh.

This particular dog unfit, a throwback to the lurcher-collie stock it had been reclaimed from, and so passed on to the son of a tenant, but in truth much closer to the guard dogs of this fortress than its pedigree brother and sisters. Were a ghost staring down into the scream-tightened hollow he would have known this grey dog, its size and conformation, familiar to his own time and chasing, as then, not wolves or infantry but the familiar, unalterable and, as now, fey-blooded hare. The scream runs through history and might summon a ghost.

The child of the petty king who set up this fortress looked out from these walls and understood only power, its finite, concentric grades which might spread or contract or be breached, like ripples, himself for the moment its hub and, so, blind. The walls gleaned from and imposed upon the landscape so long ago that they have become it again, the stones reverting to their old stock, lichened and weathered, the ruin itself never still as by fern-root and frost-leverage it moves with the landscape's face, still used at shearing time to pen sheep, as it was built from the first as much to hold stock as men, borrowed from to patch its own rents and gateways or to mend the stone fences which shaped the land to a later sense of order, a lesser containment since the fences were raised as much to clear pasture and arable as to hold in or out and gesture at squares and rectangles, not circles, and are now of the land themselves, set aside by electric fences, and weather and shift too, insensibly, and echo, in their mortarless, bird-sheltering postcard quaintnesses, the work of the giants or princelings in the lonely long age of iron.

The poets and priests of that age taught that all things flow, and that change is essence, and so things stay the same. The boy and his dog, each with his muddled and surfacing bloodlines, set out in a land where time and place interweave and cannot be unravelled, or cut. It is no desert of ice or sand or buried alluvia – the dry extremes where a skull may lie waiting for explorer or archaeologist, scarcely marked by the elements – it is land that's both stomach and surface, digesting itself forever between stone and water, changing them even, the will of the soil to choke up waterways, the will of the water to freeze and abrade the rocks till the rocks become earth. Not earth enough said Cromwell to bury a man, not water enough to drown him, no tree to hang him, the next thing to Hell, where death is impossible.

It could be the Hare with its six year lifespan is the one unchanged presence in this seeming immutable landscape. The Hares which limped in as the forest retreated, the Greenwood that stood and fell before these walls were imagined, that ghosts the place insensibly because man and beast walk without knowing it through the spaces vacated by oak and red pine, rowan and holly and thorn and kept vacant by the hill sheep who have no need for the men that own and imported them but graze and lamb unshorn and often die with their faces in moorland streams and whose grazing forbids the resurrection of the forest which lingers, among its own ghosts, in trees like the twisted thorn by the red boulder where the spring breaks out, as seedlings fortressed by stone heaps or clefts, and armored besides like holly and thorn, or on islets immune from sheep in the tarns that mirror the moorland sky or in bogholes that men have cut through two millenia, taking fuel from the bog, burning the land itself, the slow drowned debris of the lost forest, the reclaiming heather and furze, so that one tree in this landscape stands out and holds in itself the potence of 20,000 trees and their ghosts.

The tree by the spring more potent still, from the dues paid it over the centuries by the mothers and daughters of the townland, no taller than the boy who peered through its leaves and believed by the tenant farmers to be the same tree always, though nine had sprung from the crevice below the red boulder since the walls were built, self- or bird-seeded, always a white-

thorn gnarling slowly above the small pool which had fed and
determined the site of the fortress, its successor a whip-shoot
already by its roots.

The women came here in dread of travail, their own or their
cattle's, with red scraps torn as offerings from their petticoats'
hems. The scream shivered through the leaves at the boy's face,
trembling a few bleached threads, still pink, that clung to a
branch. Somewhere in the mud of Flanders a leaf from this tree,
folded for protection into a sweetheart's clumsy letter, dissolved with the man whose blood coursed in the boy's veins.

If, when the moment was broken, the dog drank at the spring,
a wisp of hair, its own or its quarry's, may have scudded upon
the surface, a minute tincture of blood may have mixed with
the pulse of the spring where on parched summer evenings the
unalterable forebears of the hare had drunk and been mirrored.
The ripples would spread from the grey dog's muzzle, buck-
ling the sky and the stone and the tree, with the boy above him,
hare dangling from his hand, his face at the heart of the ripple,
invisible, and to him looking down, the dog-mirror broken up
too.

The boy with his hand on the red boulder defined the scream's
radius. The sound was absorbed, the echo stillborn and therefore unended. The granite, erratic in this limestone world, too
hard to work, too massive to shift, too slick to sharpen axe,
sword or scythe upon. Here before the lost forest or the walls,
lichen-free too except where it's lapped by the sheep-cropped
turf, yet infinitesimably changing into the land's face, the
platelets of mica prised off by frost, the crystals within it surfacing, baring the lattices through which they receive light and

sound, which record and perhaps transmit the scream and its burden.

Otherwise, just a fragment of memory in the mind of a man an ocean and a continent away. His eyes now are pale, disabused; his hair dry and short, the red faded almost to grey. He walks stiffly on the shaded side of the street between his boarding house and the Chinese diner where he gets his lunch. Whatever he thinks or remembers, he must filter through the tramlines and wires, the traffic, the blending of asiatic and aboriginal voices, the odour of cheap fruit and exhaust.

He moves beneath the department store awnings, invisible on the street as most people here are – incurious human habits, like shadows. He has left his sweat in five of the country's ten provinces, left a little blood too, fighting like his grandfather for one foreigner against another, on a third foreigner's soil. After a life of ships and railroads he knows and cares less about anything than the boy he was.

But that moment is one of his touchstones; he comes back to it once in a while, walking beneath the unnoticed backdrop of rooftops and mountains, and more especially in the hour before sleep in his room on the second floor, filtering the sounds through the walls and the open window.

Not very clearly. It's a though the screen of his inner eye were fissured, unwilling to come together. He knows that place in his cells, but can never complete the picture.

It is mixed out of the light hill wind, and the dog whose name he remembers still; the death of a hare, its cry somehow linked to a loose thread, streaming from the branch of a thorn bush. That and the dear, vital smell of the place, which he reaches for in his brain but seems to have lost forever.

The scream, all the same, remembers the boy precisely. It is a testament *in extremis*, uniting things: less a harmony than a current which found a conductor in everything.

Perhaps it is on that wavelength that the angels ply.

The Teacher

*T*he teacher answered the knock at the back door and his mother-in-law pushed past him, calling her daughter's name. His father-in-law stared out at the crossroads, drumming his fingers on the car roof. The engine was running.

The teacher turned back to a house that felt gaunt with disaster. His wife's voice was unnaturally high, on the stairs, hurrying the children.

She must have been packed and waiting. Her mother came down with the big suitcase, holding the little boy. She turned the child's face away from him as she passed, and swept up the waterford vase, at the same time, from the kitchen table.

His daughter marched by, tense-shouldered, her eyes on the door. Her mouth was set in a miserable smirk.

His wife stood in the hallway, with the matching blue samsonite bags. She set them down, and her eyes scanned the kitchen. An ugly grief began to lay hold on her face. She bent almost into a squat to take up the luggage again. Her look was momentary – defiant and unforgiving: he could see no trace of dilemma there.

All he could think to do was to help with her bags. She tugged away from him.

He stood on the second step while they loaded the car. His father-in-law straightened up, as though he were called on to speak. "You've yourself to blame" he said, eyes brutish with fear and resentment. "We warned you." He spoke loudly, as if for the record, as if there were an audience.

His mother-in-law turned back in a whispering fury: "You could run" she said "but if you care one shred for your family, you'll stay." Intolerance pinched her words: "Make it clear that they left, that they'd given up on you." He saw the worst of his wife in her eyes, the stranger she had become in the last two years.

He watched the little boy's profile, at his mother's shoulder, in the rear window. She looked straight ahead, his daughter slumped in the seat beside her.

The car raised the summer dust as it turned through the gate. The dust pursued it through the crossroad. He could see it two miles away even, not the car but the dust, speeding along the concession.

His dog crept from under the porch. She brought him back to himself, stranded on the back steps with his lips idiotically parted, his eyes unnoticing.

"I don't know" he confided, and stooped and fondled her neck. She leaned against him. She felt the heat badly, her tongue lolled and dripped. She was due any day, too – her teats were hard, they leaked on his fingers.

"Did we feed you today?" he asked. It was something to do. "I'll be back" he said, and went in to the kitchen.

When his wife had picked up those bags, he'd watched with a puzzled clarity. It was not just the strangerhood, it was a kind of withering, a meanness of flesh and spirit. It had amazed him. She had cut him out of herself.

He hadn't seen the samsonite bags together since their honeymoon.

The kitchen was neutral. The last few minutes had left no more impression upon it than any few minutes in the last 90 years. There were already no echoes.

Yet it was absurd to pass his hand through the space where she stood, and stooped for the cases – the knees, the arms that were his once – and deny she had been there.

He opened the cellar door, and went heavily down the stairs. Fear. It lay behind all the new masks of belief, enlightenment, outrage. And god knew, he was fearful himself. "I'm scared" he said out loud. The basement air was dead.

He scooped out a tin measure of dog food from the bin.

The Glory was waiting behind him, on the stairs.

He stepped up into the sunshaft, and remembered. It came from the kitchen window and filled the stairwell, just as it had last winter and stopped him dead, with his armful of stove-wood.

It changed everything. How could he have forgotten it? He stood again, suffused with Grace, the radiant gentleness of the Creation.

He stood till the Glory passed. Then fumbled his way up the stairs.

He thought, he could have found this each afternoon, in the months since he'd been dismissed.

No. The Glory found you, the wind bloweth where it listeth, you couldn't go looking for Grace. Or lie in wait for it.

He went back on the porch and set down the collie's food. But she only sniffed at it, and followed him round to the barn. He threw down some hay for the lambs: they were putting on weight, their widow's peaks had grown dense and fleecy between their pink eyelids. "I'll be breeding youse in September" he told them, using the farmer's dialect, persuading himself of a future. The big rooster was up on the crib, gargling in agitation, its hysterical sham of masculinity. One of the mother bantams, with fifteen chicks at least, came running at his boots, wings akimbo, tail menacingly flared. He laughed, and backed off. He loved the banties, they were almost wild birds.

He went round to the biffy and sat there, with the door open to the pasture. His refuge since springtime. The stack of books, the hoarded magazines. His fingers itched for the news, but he'd come to dread the little radio. He sat on the edge of the seat, taking stock. How his world had shrunk, when the odours of whitewash and quicklime and shit, his shit, in this shaky outhouse, were the breath of freedom.

"I just don't know" he said, again. The collie looked up from her patch of shade. When you stopped talking to your wife, then your children, that left the animals. "No" he said, reaching down his twenty-two from the rafter-hook, "You stay here, girl. It's safe. No one's going to hurt the farm."

He pocketed a handful of shells and set off down the fenceline. Over his shoulder the skewed shadow of the barn was creeping up the sandhill pasture. An obelisk shape which would reach the hill's crest, and match it exactly, on June 12th and July 4th each year. No, no one would hurt the farm, not this time around. But he'd had his own visions. One hundred acres, in two acre parcels, a shack on each plot. He always imagined the peasants – there'd be a *village* on his farm – as oriental, or south american. It made sense. But what time-frame?

Wheels, he thought, wheels turning. A glimpse of the fall of empires suddenly, here, in his sunlit acres. His own shadow ran to his left, stretching, vaulting, recoiling to the land's contours.

It was absurd. He had never been an original thinker, he'd got by. He had some knowledge, but little understanding. The knowledge was all that he wished to pass on. And he had no courage, no easy convictions.

"I'm weak" he told himself, and *Gentle Jesus weak and wild* came out of nowhere. Only two years ago, there'd been nothing you could not mock.

At the crown of the warren above the creek a big groundhog stood bolt upright, on sentry duty. He slipped in a single shell and sighted at the base of the creature's dark skull-cap. The collie whimpered excitedly. He lowered the gun. "Go home, I told you, Stop following me." She didn't believe him. She went twenty paces and sat, tongue lolling, waiting. "Go on" he said "I mean it. Home!" She went slowly, belly low to the ground, watching him over her shoulder.

When you stopped talking to the animals, that left the ghosts. He ejected the shell and let it lie where it fell. He climbed through the fence, and the wires twanged down the field. Just over the creek was his favourite spot: a hedge-bottom full of old apple trees. He'd an intimate sense of the presences here, though no one had any record or memory of a house and there was nothing, except the apples, to hint at it. But he knew in his heart that a couple had lived here, in harmony, had cleared a homestead from the Queen's Bush, before the fields and the dikes and the groundhogs.

He'd come here and tell them new things. The birth of his daughter, fifteen years back. His father's death. The new barn roof. His son.

When his daughter was six she'd come over the creek and said she'd seen someone there. "An old man" she said "under the apple tree, smoking a pipe." And "I think it was God" she said "he disappeared."

His wife had laughed fondly. She had always laughed fondly back then, she could afford to. At his tags of quotations, his funny ideas, his trust. Her laughter was bitter these days.

Six months ago he had stood here and rested from splitting wood, and the creek had been full of snow, its ten foot banks obliterated. And over the snow were the tracks of the night creatures. The snowshoe hares, the skunks, the raccoons. And one amazing series of finger scoops, three feet apart, in pairs, like angel wings, and no other track between. The wing tips of an owl, brushing the snow.

He suddenly thought of the Rough Beast's spoor, crossing the township, crossing the land. What could he say to his ghostly friends? It was not their trouble. He turned towards the path up to the woodlot. When you stopped talking to the ghosts, that left yourself.

Someone was shouting. He could see dust clouds beyond the sandhill pasture, and vehicles crowding their barnyard. The house was still out of sight. He heard voices again, and there were three figures running along the crest of the pasture. They carried guns. One of them pointed and headed down towards the creek. The collie came out of the hayfield and raced beside him.

The teacher stood for a moment; without knowing why, he brandished his rifle. He could not believe this; it wasn't until he started to run that the fear came true. He splashed through the swale below the path, and dodged round the ruin of the sugar shack, under the trees.

In the mud before him was the print of a young deer. He propped the rifle against a maple trunk and dropped on one knee. His knuckles fitted exactly into the slots. The cool mud welled up to his finger-webs. The freedom of the woods.

He left the gun, and ran on through knee-high ash seedlings, and the blue-green switches of silverthorn that rasped at his clothes.

There was shouting to his right. The mosquitoes came up in a cloud as he skirted the little slough at the heart of the wood, and he doubled back, across the woodmen's trail, and threw himself down by the sheaves of timber-tops left from the winter. He crawled in where the branches hung over a knoll, and lay still.

He had always been a good hider. Often the other kids gave up, even went home, before he came out of cover.

His heart settled down. A chipmunk raced along a branch just above his face, oblivious. The world was so still. He felt in that moment that he was back in paradise. The details of things close up to his eyes were enough for a lifetime. The light and smell of the woods.

This was the mode of his hide-and-go-seek days. When waiting was not suspense, but a calm fitting in to your refuge. A mental camouflage. It was like hibernating – and when they gave up and went home you had, with reluctance, to rouse yourself, climb out of your lair, and walk back, lightheaded, into the world.

His heart kicked back in him. Someone was standing close by, on the far side of the woodmen's trail. The light was behind the figure – he could see the gun, sense the jittery watchfulness. Somewhere, back through the trees, he could hear the underbrush being trampled. So a deer must feel – but they thought he still had his rifle.

The hunter turned, with his gun, and his profile showed against a gap in the trees. He moved two paces and turned again. Oh god, that stolid, good-hearted farmboy. He had never got much from the school, he had done his time, without much resentment. In the summer they'd worked together, loading the haymow, combining the corn. There'd been enough respect, both ways.

"Logan" he said "I'm here. Don't call out."

The boy swung around, his features washed out again by the backlight. The gun jabbed nervously.

It was bearable with the young. If history turned over again, they'd find ways to forgive themselves.

He did not know how well the boy could see him. "It's a terrible thing that's happening, Logan" he said. He mustn't say too much; it could hurt, down the road.

"Come out" the boy said. "Come out and stop talking."

"Leave me be, Logan" he said. "If you don't, I shall shoot you."

He was staring at a lichen scale, on a twig, just a few inches from his boot. It was like the skin of a frog, it was utterly fascinating.

"Come out of there" the boy said. His voice bullied and pleaded. "Will you just get the hell out of there." His nerve broke and he shouted out: "Here, he's here! I've got him — quick!"

There were answering shouts, they echoed in the enclosed air. Branches whipped and snapped.

"You shouldn't have done that, Logan" the teacher said, and he reached down quickly as if for his rifle. It was the lichen, though, that he needed to touch. It was like feeling in the dark for a glass on the table, something your eye had located before the light was turned out. He was human enough still that his eyes had to lift to the boy's.

The last thing he saw was not the brief lap of flame from the shotgun's muzzle. It was Logan's body, nudged open by jigsaw fissures, burning from within; and the orange coals there made porous the trunks of the maple trees, too, as though a sunrise were penetrating the whole world's fabric.

He sees it still. The coals are unconsumed.

The Glass Sphere

*T*he glass sphere had drifted on the Pacific for almost two hundred years. It had gone so far south that the ground swell of the Hawaiis had drawn it in, but then a southwester drove it back to the open sea and it went with the currents, northwest, riding high on the surface, entering wave troughs and skimming the swells and rollers, light as a sea bird.

The birds had ridden it, too. Gulls, terns, and once – a thousand miles from land – an exhausted storm petrel, one of those brown life-sparks which American whalers called Mother Carey's chickens and believed were the souls of drowned seamen.

For years at a time it had been host to barnacles; their miniature atolls of lime had altered its balance, so that the boss of its closure had lifted clear of the water and it had spun anti-clockwise. The barnacle colonies came and went; they left crusts on the glass like faint, cryptic lettering – *U*'s, *C*'s and *O*'s.

It had ridden the verge of a warm current, a wide ocean road for migrating fish and aimless flotsam like itself. It had bobbed past a bleached wooden boat where a stiff hand dangled and brushed against it, and dead eyes stared from the gunwales into its mirroring skin.

The light of the sun, moon and stars shone milky-green through it. In a kelp-raft below Alaska it had been for a season the plaything of sea otters, lounging in seaweed hammocks as they preened and suckled.

And for nearly two years it was beached up in the Aleutians, nudged further by every tide up a thin shell beach to a cleft in the basalt cliffs. The sun and salt had lustred its flanks with ir-ridescent streaks. One dawn the sea crept in utter silence to the top of the island, carrying the glass sphere up through the trees, and then it withdrew in a fury, tearing the forest down with it, and for half the day a nest of young eagles had floated behind the sphere, till the nest disintegrated.

The sphere had frozen, and baked. The air inside it, which was the breath of a man, had made frost-flowers upon its walls, and had filled it with mist.

At the start it had been one in a chain, buoying a net between rudderless fishing junks, caught in a squall with a full catch. One boat had had time to cut itself loose, and had watched its partner dragged by the weight of the net into the wind's face and under the waves.

The boat fell slowly, the net pluming up behind it, into the stillness a furlong below the storm, leaving the colors of red, orange, yellow, suspended in that blue silence by the mass of dead fish and the glass spheres, and by the body of one of the sailors which had floated up into the net.

They hung there, lifting and sinking for almost a month, till the great grey fishes came, tearing into the swollen net. One of them got itself trapped and its death struggles ripped a whole skein of the net free. The catch floated back to the surface, the weight of the dead shark joined that of the boat and they slipped together, with the ruin of the seine, faster away from the light. A last strand of the net broke free, and the sphere that was bound to it flew to the surface, the pressure slackening inside it like the lungs of a desperate swimmer. It floated again, under a cloudless sky, trailing a rag of meshes.

The shawl of netting became a world, sustained by the glass - sphere. Algae, then weeds, then molluscs and fingerling fishes lived wholly within its shadow, feeding each other and multiplying, suspending their eggs and shells from the weakening fibres. Beside and below moved the golden-eyed, watchful predators. The sphere lay heavier in the water, dragged at by colder currents, immune now to the shifts of the wind, till the netting rotted and that world fell away to extinction. The sphere rode high again, skating before the winds.

An infinitesimal orb on the ocean's face, it was almost inviolate. Minute abrasions, small shifts in refraction and texture, a milkier light. In the law book of western physics the sphere is as much a liquid as the sea that it drifts upon. In that book the windows of Chartres and York are in flux, they pour like still waterfalls between their frames, through the centuries, achieving such magical shades and harmonies as their makers could not have imagined.

But whether the sphere's creator would have accepted, or understood, the rules of our science is unknown. His touchstone was an obsidian blade, washed out from the bank of the Yalu; its formal design and refractive perfection were a message and consolation to him from the first glass-breeders. He was master of his craft but to him glass was nature transformed and re-stated, and the art was in permanence, not change. His physics, and chemistry, were the suspension of Time and to harness that science and matter to a thing like a fishing-float was for him, degradation.

He lived in the prison of exile. The barbarians had come, as they'd come in each generation since his great grandfather's father, the atelier's founder, had watched Hideyoshi's armada in rout off Pusan. In the third year of his own mastery, he saw the atelier burned and the village with it. Saw the nose and ears of his Lord paraded down to the shore on a leather cushion, and was chained himself, with the porcelain makers, the ivory-carvers and jewellers, in the hold of a ship and brought to the land of borrowed manners and clothes, a bastard language, un-speakable food. Here where they worshipped power and ghosts, he was put to work.

The noble Satsuma who owned him was in debt to a mer-chant. The glassmaster went with a daughter, as part of her dowry, to discharge the debt.

His dreams were a vacuum; his grandfather's hands ap-peared to him no more. From dawn till the last watch he walked among labourers, debt-slaves with minimum talent, overseeing the vats of cheap, molten glass, trying to teach consistency in a place where the glass was blown into moulds. His life was an insult, but unlike the barbarians he feared his own death.

He dreamed, but they were empty daydreams. His son might be living yet, his owner might be persuaded in time to open a fine-glass workshop. He was aging and broken in spirit, he wondered sometimes if he had forgotten – if six generations of craft and judgement had died in him while he still lived.

The merchant cared only for property, and the growth of his fishing fleet, but he had no pretensions and he honoured success. He was shrewd, too, and guessed at the glass-master's anguish. Trade for the moment had overridden hostilities with Korea; he made enquiries.

One evening in March, when the larch buds were scarlet and the wolfbane had turned the headlands yellow, the merchant's son called the old foreman to his office. He held out a letter. It came from the master's wife, in the hand of a scribe for the women of his class pretended illiteracy. The young man watched as he read, and saw nothing. The glass-master bowed slightly, thanked him, and returned to the foundry.

His son and his grandson were dead. He breathed in the stench of the place, the coals and the schist-tainted glass, the sweat and the rice wine; for a moment, by the young merchant's window, he had smelled the Spring.

He snatched the blowpipe from the hands of the laborer nearest him and twirled its end through the surface of the vat. He took a great breath; all that was in his heart at that moment was grief and rage; he blew through the iron pipe.

Some of the laborers there would deny what they'd seen; others, in time, embroidered the truth. The man who had yielded the blowpipe would never forget, though. The old Korean had blown out a perfect float, without need of a mould, had walked down the gangway and plunged the sphere into the whale-oil vat, had fished it out with his hand and, after holding it up to his face, had thrown it down. It had not broken. He had come back and returned the pipe, without taking his eyes off the door at the end of the warehouse, and had gone out into the street. He was not seen again.

He did not die, though his mind might be said to have died. He disappeared into the floating world of Kagoshima.

His breath went out and survived him, drifting through space he could not have imagined, in its prison of glass. Five generations after his abdication it lay in a cul-de-sac of the ocean, passed back and forth by the currents from Japan and California, skirting the islands of Canada, outlasting the changing jetsam of the times.

In the month of July, a mile out of Naden Harbour, a girl's hands reached down from the stern of a fish boat and lifted the glass sphere from the water. The sea dripped back from it over her wrists, her face was curved and distorted in it, it was flushed through by the red sky in the west.

The boat moved on round the headland and drifted into the bay with its engines cut. "You should see this place" the fisherman said. "I like to stop in on my way home. My grandad was born here." He was an old man himself, though wonderfully active. He might have grown heavy in his middle years, but now he'd shrunk back to something like the muscularity of his youth. The boat ran gently onto the low-tide sand. He threw out a mud- anchor and they climbed into knee-deep water. He drew breath, his elbow on the gunwale. "It's called K'ung" he said. "K'ung means *Moon* in our language." He chuckled, and hauled a sack over the side: "It means *knife*, too. Who knows?" The girl reached for the blankets and clutched them to her chest. They waded ashore.

All she could see were the tumbles of moss-cloaked logs among the spruce trees, and two bleached houseposts, with animal-human faces, sagging above the sand. There was a fire-blackened ring of stones below a projecting branch, and a stack of wood at the tree's base. She threw down the blankets and stretched. "Its so good to be back on land" she cried "out in the open." She jogged on the spot for a moment, shaking her wrists out loosely. "And *this*" she said, twirling around "god, this must be the most peaceful spot on earth!"

The fisherman squatted by the stone-ring, building a tent of kindling from his sack. "A lot of people died here" he said. He was matter-of-fact, there was no reproof. She came and stood over him: "After we came, the whites, you mean?" He put a match to an old cigarette pack under the sticks. "Uh huh" he said, squinting against the smoke, "Disease and all that, you know. It was Scarlet Fever mostly." As the fire licked upwards the light seemed to die from the sky, and the trees closed in. "Are they all buried here?" the sticks crackled, her voice seemed hushed. Their shadows were flat against the trees and the housepost faces, dancing up with the flames.

The man poured some water into his billy can. "Surely" he said, and grinned up at her: "There's skulls and bones all over, best watch where you walk!" He gestured for her to pass him some logs from the pile. "There's a gravestone or two, as well, but they're Swedes."

"Swedes?"

"Hmm. There was a whaling station here, for thirty years. After the people gave up on the village. We called them Swedes but they come from Norway I believe. They went home for the winter, I guess – just a little world of their own here, never got around." He brushed his hands on his thighs. "And so some of them died here."

It was not cold but she squatted and held out her hands to the flames. "Don't matter to us" he said, with one of his droll, teasing faces: "Us Haidas come back again a few times, I told you that. Everyone got his *Hoontz*."

"Reincarnation?" she nodded. "*His* hoontz? Only the men?"

He laughed to himself, a sort of benign, soft cackle. "Ohh, ladies too. We are a very advanced people!"

"But look" she said "there's a light on the boat." He turned and squinted down the beach: "Now what could that be?" he said. "Ohh, I reckon it's that fishing float of yours, catching our firelight." She stirred up the fire, and watched the answering flare above the water. "It looks like an eye" she said "Do you find a lot of them?" He nodded: "Used to be; not so much anymore. I guess those Japanese using plastic now. Those bleach jugs do the job just as good."

"I think I'll go for a swim" she said, and stood up. "Okay?"

"It's safe" he said. "I'll heat up some grog while you're out."

Out of sight down the shore she took off her clothes and waded in. The tide had come in a little, the boat was shifting on its chain. The glass ball at the stern winked up and down. The water felt silken and safe, she was aware of the sweat and fish-grease, the fumes of the cabin from two months at sea drifting away from her on the surface. She swam round behind the boat and clambered over the side, got a towel and a clean sweater from the cabin, and came back to shore on her back, kicking lazily through the shallows, keeping the cloth dry.

The smoke was blowing towards her as she came to the fire. He looked up at her, took in the long sweater, almost to her knees, and held out a cup. "Sit next to me, girlie" he said. She hesitated – in the nine weeks she'd crewed for him, for all the jokes she'd put up with from the guys on the packer's barge, he had never made a pass, or a suggestion, or even looked at her that way.

She sat beside him, towelling her legs, huddled in front of the fire like a child. The mug of hot rye and sugar was innocent as cocoa. "There were ten big houses" he said "Dancing, feasts. And all of the food that we needed – right here." The sweep of his hand embraced the whole bay behind her.

"It must have been paradise" she said.

"It was good, yes. But people died then, too; people was hurt. People is people" he said. His hand touched her knee and began to caress it in little strokes, just the fingertips. They moved down, lifting her calf muscle, came back over her knee. She looked down at the hand, dark upon her thigh. "Were you ever with a white woman?" she said.

"Ohh" he laughed quietly, and took back his hand. "I'll not talk such foolishness with a lady like you." Back on shore, and on the ice-barge, he spoke pretty much like the other fishermen, but here he'd slipped into the near monotone of the older natives, hypnotic and lisping between the tide-lap and the settling coals.

"A lady!" she laughed, awkward now.

"Sure" he said "You are getting an education."

"Oh come on!" she said. He held up his hand: "Now don't act ashamed of that" he said "That *would* be foolishness." The hand fell back upon her thigh.

He was very gentle. She leaned back on her elbows, her eyes were closed. His voice was as soft as his touches: "We didn't lose near as much as it looks. We keep going" he said. "The changes are part of us too."

And then, "You are a smart girl, a pretty girl" he said, and turned over and lay on his side. Out at sea he had lain, stretched out in his bunk, on his back, lightly snoring; now he curled in like a child, hands thrust between his knees, his breathing inaudible. Yet she realised, almost at once, that he was asleep. He could have had her, and he left her. She would remember all of her life what did not happen.

She finished her drink and reached for one of the blankets. She lay on her back for a while, while branches shifted and fell in the forest, the sea hushed towards them, the anchor chain rasped. There was a mockery somewhere, hidden from her, like the faces up on the housepost she could no longer see.

He gave her a small slate carving he'd done on the boat. A bear with her two, human cubs. It sat on the shelf above her bed in the residence, with her other summer trophies. A vase full of eagle feathers, an orange and yellow agate, the green fishing float with its barnacle runes.

The day after registration her boyfriend got back from hockey camp. They could scarcely wait for each other. Down the hall co-eds were shrieking and a dozen competing musics boomed out at the afternoon. They tugged off their clothes, laughing, rolling upon the bed. They could scarcely wait.

She thought, in the moment before he entered her, that she'd keep the old fisherman to herself. She was starved of this; it was strangely flagrant, and private too, making love while people ran shouting past her door and danced on the grass outside.

Here it came at last. She was both in control and beyond it. She was running, backwards, up the mountain, the valley beside it rolled over upon her. "Oh jesus" she cried, and her left hand flew from her lover's shoulder. It struck the shelf over their heads, the vase teetered and fell. Eagle feathers came down in a sheaf on their faces.

The glass sphere rolled from the shelf and dropped, from the pillow to the floor. A quick, high note rang back from the walls. The glass sphere shattered. The girl gasped for breath.

The Medium

The medium can smell juniper smoke, and this confuses her because there was a place in her childhood (her mother's illness, her uncle's farm) which was filled with these eye-smarting fumes. But though smell, she knows, is time's most potent unraveller, she knows too that the sudden aroma comes not from her memory but from the narrow shard of porcelain in her left hand.

It is part of the neck and flared rim of a small jar. A knife-shaped sliver which buckles near its point. Her fingers pore at the glaze and the strange, consistent flesh of the china. The vessel recreates itself in her hand. Square-sided, high-shouldered, an austere grey pattern painted along its base. It is precious, she knows, but invisibly flawed by vanity. A clay light as air, harmonious as wind-chimes, informed by two set of hands, two memories.

She scents fraud streaming out with the sweet eddies of

smoke. Concealment, imposture, ambition. A man, not young but young in his craft, unwilling to wait for glory.

It cannot be this Yankee in front of her.

He is too big for the room. He squats against the wall, by the door, looking up at her across the table, and at the girl who brought him. His teeth are wide and white; his forearms, pink from the sun, are broad as the girl's thighs, as her own. Stooping through the door, he brought into the house the smells of soap and some western perfume. Less strong than the juniper. His eyes are pale blue. From Kanada the girl says.

The medium's hair and shoulders stand out against the paper blind behind her. The floating candle, dim as a night light on the table, picks at her features. Her cheekbones, her pale lips, the gleam of her eyes when she looks over at the girl. Unearthly.

The low room is rank with camphor, with their sugary cooking-oil, with the garbage burning at the end of the street outside. The candle light is yellow, the blind on the window, green.

"I speak, she explain you" says the medium. Her voice is surprisingly deep. Perhaps it is her awkwardness with the language, but she speaks sternly, showing no wish to cajole him. He nods. She is talking already, rapidly to the girl.

"Tell him this" she says "because it's not going to make any sense to him. He gave me something that does not belong to him. It's Korean." The girl translates, speaking softly, a question in her voice. "Or," the medium lifts her hand above the flame, "will he give me something of his own?"

The man has settled down upon the floor. His hands hang over his knees, his head lolls against the wall as he takes in the girl's words. He told her this afternoon that he was tired, that he had just got back from the mountains and was flying home in the morning. He was hard to talk with. He did not want to do the usual things. If only he were American. "You got some-tink you like a lot, gotta lonk time, okay? Same like my turkoise I sow you." She touches the chain on her neck. "Sometink like, you give her, okay?"

But he smiles: "No, she's right. I found it where the old village used to be, at Knum – you tell her that's fine, I…" but the medium cuts him off. "No speak" she scolds "busy, busy." Her head jerks: "What does he want? Didn't you explain?" The girl shrugs: "He understands. I think he *wants* you to tell him about that thing." And she checks with the foreigner: "You wanna lady tell about tink you give her, right?" He nods.

The medium sighs "You make tea now" she says "And tell him sit still and be quiet." She leans back in her chair.

He cannot tell in this light if her eyes are closed, beneath pallid lids, of if they have rolled up into her head. She has sunk into something grotesque. Clutched tight around his porcelain keepsake, her hand lies next to the bowl where the candle floats.

The girl stands in the tiny alcove, the mat held open by her body. Everything miniature: the stove into which she blows holds maybe two lumps of charcoal; the plastic jug, the wicker-sheathed teapot would do for a child's games. He's felt clumsy and overgrown from the moment he landed in Korea, and pink, coarse-skinned.

He watches her, looking for hints of her grandfather. The skin maybe darker, the eyes a touch closer together, maybe not. How does she live, he wonders. Are they hookers, the girls at the bus station? Maybe a conduit for foreign currency, shielded by the police. The taxi driver said nothing, did not look in his mirror.

And when he got paid in Canadian, his eyes lingered on the greenbacks in the billfold.

"Me American too, okay" she'd cried, pushing her way towards him. She took his arm, staking her claim. "Grandfather G.I., Marine, number one." In the taxi she'd shown him the pendant round her neck, exposing her small breasts. "He love my mother good, send dollar, radio." A rough turquoise, clasped in thin silver. "Apache" she said, her face close to his, "Geronimo, right!"

All he could think of were late night movies, and a poster somewhere of the old chief, squaw-faced, kneeling with his rifle. "Roper" she said was his name. Lopez, perhaps. In the soft locatives of Korean, *his* name has become, in the last six months, "Yollance".

She brings the teapot and two stacked thimble-cups to the table. The fortune-teller has not moved at all. Next to the girl's orange tank top, compared to the semi-uniform of the Pyongyang women, she could come from another century.

The tea is colourless, a tired lemon bouquet. The girl lifts her cup in silence, but in the gay pose of a beer commercial. Her hopeful eyes are too difficult for him.

The medium is not drinking. The shard gives off a smell now of roots, fallen walls, decay. And before that, fire – destruction. Now that first fire again – her eyes open, she peers through the juniper smoke, breathing out. The candle wavers.

She clears her throat. This will not be easy. The man has no questions, and this thing which he gave her to hold ... she needs to go into its world, as she would with a native, and have him eavesdrop and learn what he can. This will be difficult. She talks to the swaying base of the candle.

"There is one light" she says. "Shadows of hands in the rafters. A room with a white floor. He is awake while the others sleep. He should not be here. The lamp is shielded, no one must know. And it is hard for him to concentrate, so hard that his heart trembles."

The girl nods. She pours more tea as she translates, her voice by contrast light and soft, her eyes watchful. It means nothing to her, but that is not her concern. She wishes this could be the man to take her away. To the things that he takes for granted. But he does not want her body, even; she knows, sadly, that this is not the man. Not even American. He stares at her mouth and eyes, trying to understand.

"He make bowl" she says next. "Make again bowl he bweak before. Ty to make good like first time, like bowl his ..." her eyes drift to the door, she fumbles at the language, mutters an English word or two to herself, then brightens, triumphant: "his *boss*, yes, boss make bowl yesterday, okay?" The man nods, frowning. "He dop it, tis guy" she explains. "Now he make fix it. In night time, yemember."

The voices go back and forth. One speaks, one watches, one listens. One speaks, one listens, one tries to suspend the vision and clutches the keepsake, fighting off thought or distraction while the blue smoke of memory threatens to overwhelm her.

The hands of the potter are slippery. The wheel begins, stroked around evenly by his left foot. The shoulders of the jar start to rise through his palms.

This is too simple not to be real, at least in *their* minds. So shabby and matter of fact in its ritual. Has she really tapped in, he wonders, to the old world of Knum. Knum, pillaged and burned by Hideyoshi's marines; no single master remembered by name out of ten generations or more: just the word *Knum*, a set of techniques that have never been mastered, maybe twenty authentic pieces in the world's museums.

The woman's voice is monotonous, slow. If Roh were here now, his shadow for five months – interpreter, watchdog, in the end a wistful, confiding friend. Or any one of the potters he's studied with, their village founded two centuries back near the old site, what would one of the *them* learn, if there *is* something to be learned. To them the old potters of glorious legend are a sort of guardians, spirits of place, almost angels, who came before and mined the saprolite pocket – if it ever existed – in the hanging valley.

The jar dries, undetected, its grey skin blanching, from the light to the dark of the moon. With a half-dozen others it is brought by the lesser apprentices out to the workshop, and shown in the sunlight. He strives not to stare at it. One jar is rejected at once, dashed down by the Master into dust and crumbs by his feet. The floor is composed of such debris. They work together, applying the slip-glaze. The moon at its full again. The Master traces a chaste wave around half the base; stands back and watches. His assistant completes the design. The Master nods. He feels triumph tighten around his heart.

The moon is dark. The front porch of the dragon kiln is loaded, and sealed. They wait.

Two pairs of eyes, one blue, one brown, open but somewhere else. Sometimes she wearies of trying to sell her way out; if only she had the language, the dollars to *buy* her way out. A man like this, if he understood, if she had not misjudged her approach. Her shoulders droop in the silence, she can feel dejection setting in again.

She turns her head. Watches her grandmother staring down over the candle. Tonight she will go to the airport, take a businessman from the South to the Jade Flute. Her fingers pluck at her skirt.

A sudden rich laugh of pleasure, masculine, high, breaks from the medium's throat. The room leaps back into focus.

The Master beams. He stands by the window, holding the jar canted in the daylight. "This" he says "this is my masterpiece." The assistant closes his eyes. "I will show you" the Master says, stepping down, moving into the room till he is surrounded by every member of his atelier. He brings the jar up to his face, purses his lips above the flared rim. "Harmony" he whispers, and then blows.

The room is filled with a conch-cry, a distillation of wind chimes. The walls sing, the candle dips madly in its bowl, the low tone rings through their bones. The man and the girl both have tears in their eyes, without knowing it.

The merriment in the old eyes could almost be mockery. He watches the Master pluck from his sleeve a double loop of twine. It tightens upon the jar's neck. The Master stands, the jar swinging at his breast, like a player at a village dance. "Listen" he tells them; his knuckles rap the jar. The porcelain song rings out again, marrying its other self, and the laugh ripples out again with it.

They are all infected. The girl's head lifts, the man's hands shake with his laughter. The easy tears blur his vision. The Master is in the doorway, his cape thrown off, beneath it a peasant's garments. "It is all I can do" he says. "It is your time now." The assistant is holding the jar, he is watching the eyes that laugh back at him. In that moment he understands. The

Master was not deceived, nor his Master before him. It is the inheritance.

The Master takes down the wayfarer's staff from the porch. Makes a gesture of benediction through the room and is gone, an old, happy man, down the valley. The Maker turns from the door. The shame and elation confirm his mastery.

The echoes fade out. The medium raps her hand on the table. She is holding the porcelain shard towards him. He scrambles forward on one knee, to take it. It is hot from her touch. "There's no more" she says harshly. "After that it's horrible." She wipes her palm upon her sleeve. "Finis" the girl says. "Bad tink happen. Forget it, okay?" And through her, his answer: "He says the Japanese, right? He knows. They wiped them out. Is that true?" Her grandmother nods. "Now make me some tea" she says, exhausted.

They drink together in silence. The girl's hands start to fidget, she is tapping her feet, and he reaches in his pocket. "Shall I pay you or her?" he says. "Pay her, pay me" she says curtly. She wants to be gone.

He stoops in the room. "But how much?" he asks. "Here" the girl takes his billfold. There's Korean money, Canadian, American, a couple of travellers cheques. She pulls the American dollars out. He sees a yearning that is different from greed, as she stares in confusion at the almost identical bills. "One, ten, twenty" he points out the figures. She gives the fortune teller two tens: "Okay?" He shrugs, it must be a fortune, but still ... Her fingers hesitate. He takes back the money: "Here" he says. She takes the ten, folds it carefully and slips it inside her belt. She smooths her skirt and tugs at the tank top. For a moment she is offering herself, her eyes on the billfold, but she turns abruptly to the door. He is fingering the keepsake in his jacket pocket. "I bing taxi" she says.

It is still waiting, at the end of the street. He ducks back in at the doorway. "Thank you" he says "That was very good." She has not moved from her place, there is still the tiny tea cup, half full, in her hand. The faintest of smiles may, or may not, be for him. The greenbacks still lie, by the candle bowl, where the girl laid them. He reaches and takes her left hand: dry, cool, it flinches, then lies inert. "Good luck" he says helplessly. Her eyes come up to meet his. She nods, impassive.

For a minute or two she sits, tilting the cup in her fingers, watching two leaf stalks drift in the yellow tea. She is not thinking, she sees nothing else, she is waiting for the last whisper of juniper smoke to vanish. But it will not leave, she is back in her uncle's farm, under the barn roof where the hay is dusted by snow blowing in through the cracks. She is clutching a grey silk glove to her face, inhaling its perfume, muffling her sobs. A week before *he* knows, she knows that her mother, down in the city, is dead. She can guess what will be.

She sets down the tea, unfinished. The dollars upon the table are crisp and smooth, as though they had been starched and laundered. She stands up, folding them slowly, and takes them back into the alcove. When she presses the switch, the light bulb and radio come on together.

There are riots again in Seoul, and talk of reunification. Police block the streets with their clubs and shields, young people hurl flaming bottles. What can you believe? In her childhood "police" meant the Japanese soldiers.

She goes to blow out the candle. On the floor, by the wall where he was sitting, lies a small coin. She bends and picks it up. It is a button, brass, with *LEVIS* embossed around it. From the eyelet hangs a frayed loop of cotton thread, grey. She pulls it free, and the juniper smoke swarms again into her room.

She sees water through a bird's eyes, breaking softly upon sloping rocks. There are reeds, smoke from a cabin's chimney. She knows that a woman has died, far away, near America. That the man, who is really a boy, will fly home tomorrow to grief.

She holds the thread to the candle-flame. It flares and snakes at her finger tips. She drops the ash in the bowl, watches it drift and settle, licks the smart from her finger. She blows out the candle. What could she have told him, even if she had known? It would not have meant what it means. It is done so long before it is understood.

The Widow

The widow died, surrounded by gentle strangers. Their soothing voices, beneath the low-pitched ceiling, drowned out the birdsong from the garden and she found herself, out of nowhere, a cut-out, a black leaf flittering down a tunnel of light whose walls curved in and wavered around her.

It was silent, yet voices seemed to be chattering within her, agitating still more the shape which she had become.

A moth, a bat, a bird in a chimney. There were rents in the walls, but she saw only darkness. There were gaps too, from time to time, on either side, rounded like archways, but their lintels trembled and beyond there was only a black wind sucking.

And then, below her, was a different, grainier light, and she was hovering in a draught that swept down the tunnel, looking in through a smokey glass at her son's face. She could see him aslant, very close to her, huge, only the side of his face visible. He was older than she remembered, altered by private concerns. He was unaware of her, and she felt no need to reach in to him.

The wind snatched her off, and tumbled her past another dim window. A snapshot as though from a car passing at dusk. A mother and child, the child a woman already, facing each other across the room, absorbed in their worlds. The tilt of the mother's head was her daughter's.

She left them behind on the wind. She rose and fell and zig-zagged in the lightshaft, till the walls billowed out to her right, and divided, and she was standing on grass.

She stepped forward, hesitant. Under the trees was a table set with a snow-white cloth; there were glasses, decanters and glass jugs, baskets of fruit. Young people stood talking, in open-neck-ed shirts. The girls wore short dresses, their arms were grace-ful, their voices were made of laughter. And he was among them, smiling, as young as *they* were. He looked up, still smil-ing as she faltered, the same smile, not a special one for her, though his eyes did recognise. They all turned round, to include her.

But she did not want that. She was awkward still, uncertain, a little dazed, and she wanted just *him*. He was hers, after all – his welcome should have been more personal. After the first relief at seeing him, and her quick wonder at his youth – he was just what he'd been when she had met him, a world ago – she wanted them to be together, separate: she was not ready for this company, this queer springtime out-of-doors. He should under-stand.

She stood her ground. Her eyes demanded that he come to her. She was hurt, angry, and he seemed not to notice. He *would* not notice. He smiled, and the other young people smiled, the group of summer girls, and their smiles reproved her, without meaning to – for her disappointment.

She was covered with shame. He was siding with them against her, he was *one* of them. Yet he smiled, happily, in his youth and ease, smiled even as she hung her head and moved away from the glade, hurt as an outcast child, wanting only invisibility. And like a child, to her further shame, she looked back for a moment and saw them still smiling, untouched by her pain, he too. She hurried away.

What were those girls to him? Did he think that he could have done better than choosing her? She picked her way, with her misery, through an open woodland; the light and the steady breeze between the grey trunks, the leaf-canopy overhead, translucent and veined from the sunlight, the cry of birds suddenly come into focus, made the misery hard to cling to. The ground sloped before her, her feet were whispering through last year's leaves, there were hints of blue pools (of water? of bluebells?) through the trees.

She had never been here, but was somehow familiar, as though it were blended from childhood scenes, or from picture-cards come to life. She was aware at that moment of her young hands, of the effortless walking, of an almost forgotten tune humming itself in her throat. She could smell the place now, the fragrant, uncluttered breath of time past. Safe. She was wholly alone, she knew it, in this world.

And yet. Had she become a shrew after all, or a will unto herself, in their years together? An insistent, angry will that had tamed his heart? Somehow she could not remember enough. And was *he* so perfect?

She had lost him now, anyway. The cascade of shame and self-justification was stilled by this place. No one would judge her here, but herself.

She scarcely wanted to think of that life, which had been her whole life. How strange, but how simple. Like a dream that was not worth clinging to when you woke, or that you were too lazy and present-contented to retrieve. There were fields to her left through the trees, long open meadows that flanked the wood-side and went down to the edge of a lake, or river.

Between her and the scene floated an image of sharing, of marriage, as a boat on the water, two passengers facing each other. Each had a pair of oars, each pulled in the opposite direction. There was a story-book drawing of Mr. Toad, upended in his skiff, oars awry as knitting needles, his legs kicking, and she laughed, like a wise child watching the grown-ups learning to learn.

Because, of course, both partners did not row at once, except in moments of conflict. You rested on your oars, while the other took over, and you imagined or pretended that you pulled towards the same goal. But no, when it was your turn you were going back again, in your own direction, looking at where you'd been taken, or at the other's face.

She was out of the wood, looking down at the lakeshore. Alone in the field was a hollow oak tree, seamed by lightning, the ground trampled hard and black all around it by sheltering cattle. She knew this place. Yes, surely somewhere around the lake was a ruin, the grey walls of an abbey or castle. She could visualise the old courtyard, with the sunken graves of the nuns, with pigeons strutting and the cry of jackdaws. She started to walk, diagonally down the field. There was no doubt that she had become a child, or almost one.

If the course was a straight line, or even if the river twisted and wound, there was still the question. If your partner had done the more rowing, and then that partner died or left you, or was stricken with illness, or you left him, where would you be in relation to the starting post? It was like a puzzle which you had to get clear in your mind. A problem from when you first learned to do math in your head.

Did the survivor have to get back to scratch, to recover herself? Such hard work it would be to row yourself back, retracing everything. Back to front, too. She began to laugh at the absurdity, hopscotching down through the grass, because none of it mattered, here she was.

She found words to the tune she'd been humming. A thing she had learnt from the music sheets in her aunt's piano-stool. She sang it when she walked out by herself when there were not chores to do, the younger children to tend, or schoolbooks to study. A silly song, a mighty foolish song, but it had gone with her into those precious solitudes. *Fare thee well, ye Mormon Braes, Where oft times I've been cheerie, Fare thee well, ye Mormon Braes, For it's there I lost my dearie ...*

The singing brought back the dear scent of meadowsweet, and there at once were the cloud-yellow flower tufts, along the fence by the millstream. *So I'll put on the gown of green As a forsaken token And that will let the young men know That the bonds of love are broken.* "That's a frivolous song for Eileen to be learning" her mother had said, and her aunt had laughed. Her forgotten name came back, and was lost again, as she climbed the fence.

She looked down through her reflection in the stream. Waterbeetles sculled on the surface, little foam-packs clung to the rushes. Just once, at this time and place, she had believed in the wonderful safe absurdity of the world and her own aspirations. Though it was not safe, neither safe nor kind. Grief and separation, betrayal; the angels of pain, disease, madness brushing her children with their wings. But here, and then ... *So I'll go back to Stricken Town Where I was bred and born in And I'll find me a bonny new lad To marry me in the morning ...*

That was the time when you reached for experience, through guesswork and fantasy. Not *from* experience, but from stories, books, gossip, from intuitions and unsuitable songs. Were you ever so much yourself, before or after?

She sat above the water, clasping her knees to her chest. She rocked to and fro to her song, staring at the grey walls past the mill. *There's as good fish intil the sea As ever yet were taken ...* And you knew then, as she knew now, that a child, after all, could just cry herself to sleep.

The stream flowed below her, unchanged and unchanging. Its syllables merged with the commonplace words of her song. She was back to herself, completely. She stopped rocking and leaned her face on her knees. Felt the texture of the cotton dress on her cheek. Alone with herself, one heartbeat before love.

She willed her own extinction.

Hell

Hell is the desolation after a nightmare. It is lying awake in the half-dark, paralysed, with no door ajar to cry out to, no brother sleeping close by. The dream has gone, its staring images are fading down a swift corridor, but the fear intensifies, the terror does not roll back into the familiar walls. There are no walls.

A long moment. So long that you'll have been driven mad times without number before you come to realise that you are Hell.

The only escape is back into the nightmare, but when you reach you find that it has divided, and divides again endlessly, into smaller, deadlier dreams.

"To hell with this" you say, and you might be in outer space because there's no sound, no air, no echo. No one to hear, or to make a difference.

Terror, or the dreams from which you bolt – into terror. Nothing else, nothing in between.

You cannot go on like this. You have no choice.

The child cries out from his nightmare and no one comes. He cries again, and hears his mother stir, through the wall; her drowsy, questioning moan. Now what he hears is worse than what he's just woken from. The other voice, growling beside her, and "Can it, kid" high and vicious, coming straight afterwards. He hears her soothing, and he cries "Momeee", knowing he shouldn't have, he should have lain still, the voice comes again like a whip: "You little bastard, shut *up!*", it is your voice, you thought that you were the child and now you are, hearing his mother calming *your* rage, soothing and wheedling *you* back to peace, the bed creak, its head rapping the door-jamb, the cries through the wall and his fear, which is yours now, too young and total to understand hate.

The excuses won't come. You try, but the words slip away.

What the little fucker must have felt like. You didn't realise, you had no ...

But the words slip away.

You cannot go on like this.

There's noise, suddenly, light and people, their smell, oh god yes, you can remember it, the street-car stopping, you step down: wet streets, the wind blowing papers along the sidewalk. You collide with someone's shoulder, you turn and snarl. Oh *that* face. He's middleaged, alarm is killing the pale smile, he's astonished, ready to be afraid. You turn back and kick at him, curse again, then head down towards the arcade, swaggering between the passing faces. His dismayed eyes following you, it's made your day.

Blessed are the meek. Where does that come from? A tattered

poster outside the church. "Fuck *off*" you croon to yourself "I should have punched that loser out."

And you want to stay in this dream, because it's familiar, there are smells and feeling, it's home. But you can't have it, it's fading, you're that loser no, staring at your back through the crowd, you want to cry, it's awful …

Please.

The owl stares down from a branch just above you. You never liked this place, the swampy creek and the skunk-cabbage flowers, yellow as the owl's mad eyes. Bubbles are burping out of the mud, and there are other yellow flowers in clumps. The bugs eat you and get in your hair. The smell gives you the creeps, it's the sort of place a murderer would hide his victim.

Just twenty yards behind the houses.

Some of your nightmares took place here. You're holding a rope, you and – his name won't come back, he's got no face – and you're tying his sister up. She's frightened, the rope flattens her wrists to the tree. You leave her, whimpering. You got hell for that. Remember her eyes when you were leaving? They're your eyes now. God. That's what she keeps on saying, Momeee, Daddy, God. And no one comes.

"Oh fuck" you say "That's not fair – I was only a kid …" But you feel as though you are drowning.

There you are, look at you. No. *Yes*. The stupid faces you pull while you're talking. It's the dinner break, it's the donut shop by the station, it's the bar, it's the cafeteria, it's all of them. You're the people who sit with you in those places, watching and listening while you tell that story, your story which always ends up the same, however it starts: "I goes *smaack*!" and you punch your fist into your palm, in front of your face, your vicious half-moon face, someone else you've punched out, they go along with you, *you* lie here now and go along with you, and they see right through you, they're no better than you but their laughter mocks you, as you lie about punching out strangers and this will go on for ever, you and your cronies, but the cronies are gone now.

You cannot go on like this.

You pity yourself, but the dreams fade so rapidly you can't hang on to the things that you pity. You pity the people you despised, you pity everyone you hero-worshipped, or followed, or modelled yourself on.

Who were they? Here's an identification parade. Lined up. There's nobody there. Dummies made of clothes, with white socks, a few tattoos. There's no one there. "It's all shit."

There's not even an echo here. You're going to lie forever at the heart of those words and disgust: "It's all shit."

"Help me, someone." Forget it. You are so bored with yourself, it is worse than the terror, it *is* the terror. Weren't you always bored with yourself? If there *were* an echo here it would be like a far-off, remorseless heartbeat: *Bore*-dom, *bore*-dom, *bore*-dom ...

You peel off from the guys at the back door. You're like seabirds scattering in the fog, your whoops and whistles fading from each other, but you carry the warmth of the company with you. These are your people, these are your friends – you stagger and laugh at the corner: "whoo-eee" you challenge the night, knowing it's your friend too. Sure, they'd turn against you for a dime, and you'd do the same, but that's life, eh? You've got friends and you've got somewhere to go home to, someone. You're someone.

You march on, singing bits of the songs from the evening, laughing at the wisecracks you can't remember. Just as long as the bitch doesn't ruin it, with her long face. She's lucky you come home at all. God damn.

She's a dog, she's a doormat. She's as bewildered and gutless as her kid.

She loved you.

God damn. That was the only time in your life *you* were in control. And why did she want you? Why did she take it?

She loved you. Ah, love – screw it. The disappointed eyes are worse than the frightened eyes, bruised eyes … Only one pair of disappointed eyes in your whole life. She loved you.

You can only talk to yourself. Here's – his name won't come back – he could tell a story. He'd ways of putting things, he wasn't educated, but he had the words, he laughed at himself too, he wouldn't end up like this.

It's the words you need. What can you find? "Blessed are the meek", "Death before dishonor", "the whole truth and nothing but the truth", how can you think for yourself without the words? "Lest we forget."

You troop in from the yard, catching up with the guys by the library door. You nudge each other, and *you* jeer at them, suck-holes, bookworms, faggots. And one of them turns – his name won't come back – he's got rank and respect, he scares you so much you piss yourself a little, sensing your mob fade back and leave you to it, to the mercy of whatever is going to happen in the silence. He's a lifer, he's done banks, he's big. Just his quiet voice, a hit man being gentle with a punk: "Misery loves company, son."

But the words slip away.

Even your viciousness was not your own. You were not your own. "Give me a break" you cry "I don't have to take this."

Hell is the desolation after a nightmare ...

God damn, god damn.

You're crying. You're her and you're crying, you're having to watch you cursing at the door of the trailer ...

It's no great thing to admit your cowardice, there's no virtue in that. You were always a coward, it was staring you in the face. There's no judge here to be the merciful bully, there are none of the decent people you might tempt with repentance, sly weakness, conversion.

Why does it sound so hollow?

It always did.

Your damned voice cries out in this nothingness: "Let me end, let me cease to be." Are those your words? No one's listening, anyway.

Where are you now? A place like the skunk-cabbage swamp, but it's wider, it goes in forever. You are watching through a porthole. Is this something you forgot, or does it come from outside you? The place seems to be eating itself. A screaming mouse throws itself to the owl, a rabbit hastens to the fox's lips, the fish leaps into a heron's beak, the chipmunk lies down with the mink. You can hear their music through the glass. The trees plunge themselves into the swamp, the flies swarm at your eyes.

But the words slip away.

You cannot remember dying. You were never old, were you? It won't come back. Or will it, will it?

"*Try to be brave.*" Who was that? You were very small.

You weren't ever sick, even, were you?

Maybe you're not even dead.

Waking in Eden

I

All stories are ritual. They form the same pattern, and share it
with memory and love.

Tadeusz believes this without knowing it. He throws porcelain clay upon his wheel and waits another day for Helena to
come home.

The winter jasmine blossoms outside the studio window. It is
the eleventh time it has flowered since she came back into his
life, the third time since she was taken away.

Helena sits in the library, away from the windows. She has a
new parcel of books from the outreach programme. The words
and ideas she devours, shortsighted, with passion, are as unforgiving, as coy, as the material Tadeusz works with.

Her parole hearing comes in two days. It is her second. She
knows and believes that all stories form the same pattern.

A weight, a gulf, a desire.

II

To begin with. A savannah or plateau: the forest above or below, the hills, snow even, to the West. The landscape of innocence.

This is the home of Peking Man, of Australopithecus, of the yet undiscovered, undreamed of, fossil man of the Pampas.

Our man is wandering, alone. No need to have him an outcast, or utterly lost. He has wandered, simply, alone: a child on a Sunday afternoon so long that it has stretched for months.

His mind is not crowded like ours. It remarks, and remembers, everything.

Sometimes he sings to himself, sometimes the land sings through him. At night he dreams of conjunctions.

Pain is a strange kind of pleasure. Fear is a style of excitement.

He carries a weight without knowing it. He carries a stone, too – a perforated orb which spoke to him out of the world's fabric. It has grown warm in his palm.

It is itself, and him. It might become a weight for a fishnet or spindle, a missile, a fetish. It is loaded with programmes beyond his knowledge. He touches his lips to the hole in the stone. He holds it between his thighs when he sleeps.

There is a line of trees to his left. Shelter, food, the summons of novelty. Behind the trees is a canyon. Noise, energy, the river a hundred feet below surging between stone walls, down from the hills towards the forest.

The water white, and green. The canyon deeper than wide. He could throw the stone in his hand across it, easily. He will.

A gulf, a weight, a desire.

On the other side of the ravine stands a man. No, a woman.

They watch each other. They mock each other. Their mimicry becomes a dance. Without that gulf they might have run from each other, or killed, or touched too soon.

They watch each other. It is the beginning of loneliness.

The man throws the stone, which was part of him, across the ravine. To relieve his feelings.

The woman searches in the thicket, and retrieves it. Still warm from him. She holds it, smells it, tastes it.

She throws it back. Her aim is more deliberate. He catches it, bruises his finger, puts her in his mouth.

The stone has grown wings, it is a messenger, it flies back and forth across the gulf.

On the fourth day, their dance has reached its full elaboration.

On the fifth day he slips a red and yellow feather through the stone and sends it to her. She threads it into her hair, and sends him a flowering twig. The yellow buds smell of desire.

On the ninth day she is whirling the stone around her head on a length of braided grass. It whistles and hums in the air. She throws it to him, he makes the same music, the dance has become a language.

It rains for three days. They huddle across from each other, staring through the prisms of the mist, listening to the river shaking the rocks beneath them. She has the stone now. She sleeps, holding it between her thighs. They are both cold, and cold is a style of sympathy.

The rain clears, and the world is reeling with scent and color. She sends him the stone. He repairs the grass twine, ties a sweet fern-root to it, and sends her breakfast.

On the sixteenth day they sit plaiting grass across from each other, chewing the fibres, weaving with delicate, eager fingers.

With each journey the messenger's tail grows longer. It whispers across the divide.

On the seventeenth morning he throws the stone and keeps hold of its tail. She gathers the stone, and holds the rope in her teeth. He does the same. They pull the rope taut, they can feel each other hum down the line.

They learn they can strum the rope with their fingers, an armslength in front of their mouths. They share the making of music, comical, doleful; they are so delighted that they dance and strum till the line breaks, and they both fall backwards, waving their legs extravagantly at the sky, almost utterly happy.

On the twenty-eighth day the messenger's tail is attached to a vinerope, as long as the gulf is wide. It drags a cable of braided creepers, thick as their wrists. Desire has found its way.

On the thirty-first day the man walks out on a two-rope bridge. One for his feet, one for his hands. The loud snakeskin of the river squirms below him but his eyes are on her, as hers are on him. The stone has been lost, or forgotten somewhere. She hesitates to go out to him on the bridge, but her desire draws him across.

He steps from the bridge. His right hand goes to her cheek. Her right hand goes to his cheek. They are smiling. They are crying. They are shouting and dancing together.

It might be that mind and desire are the same, and that nothing may stop that leap across emptiness. It might be that mind is the weight of desire, or desire the weight of emptiness.

They comprise the story, they dream of conjunctions.

III

Helena rehearses the riddles of Xeno.

Are they more than a game for children? Is this really the root of philosophy?

She is not equipped. She hoards the encyclopedias, she always takes the table beside their shelf and piles the table with the maroon volumes. She has the big Collins dictionary, and her own English-Slovak besides. But she depends for direction on what she can get from the outreach programme.

These were her husband's favorites, therefore she tries.

He loved to air them whenever his students came round. Their Friday evenings. She had thought them a game then, too. She brought tea and vodka, and turkish sugar-cakes, and coached the children in their goodnight songs before the fireplace. It added to Anton's mystique; he depended on her.

To be one of those students. Young again, frivolous, wise in a world that seemed safe at last. She wishes she had listened more. She can smell their apartment.

It had something to do with a "number line", she can see him, his arm on the mantlepiece, explaining. His velvet jacket, that smile that came over him, as though truth and jesting were one.

A number line, how crowded it was, whether Achilles is known, in fact, to have finished the race. But she cannot apply this, somehow.

The archer looses his arrow towards the target. The arrow crosses half the distance, then half of the half remaining, then half of what's left. The halves are endless: how can the arrow ever arrive?

Was that Time or Space?

And the athlete who circles the track, through the same endless sub-divisions. Is he not, in effect, slowing down? How can he reach his goal? Is it Time that the athlete competes with, or Space?

Achilles allows the tortoise a certain handicap, and races after him. How can he ever catch him? Two moving targets? Is that Space, or Time?

What does it matter?

How could a man become a martyr for playing such games?

It vexes her mind. She turns to the dictionary.

So many "lines", though – *base-line, deadline, faultline, Green Line, mainline, party line* – this crazy, promiscuous language. "Pure line" it tells her: *A plant or animal breed in which certain characters appear in successive generations as a result of inbreeding or self-fertilisation.* How can an animal fertilize itself? Can it be true? There is nobody here to help her.

The library trusty raps on her desk: "Time's up, Jemsky. Move it!"

"I am given an extra hour, this week" she says.

The trusty shrugs and turns back to her harlequin. "Your funeral" she says.

Helena feels dizzy. She reaches for *MUN to PIC.*

IV

The wheel's harsh whisper, impelled by the stroke of Tadeusz' bare foot. He will not use an electric wheel – one more remove, through sorcery, between the thrust of his calf-muscle and the spinning plinth, the clay in his hands.

He dips his right fingers into the soft mound. A lathe of flesh. He has made a shape, now he shapes a vacancy. As always, he thinks of his fingers, two, three, in Helena's vagina.

The familiar rippling walls. Formed by her lovers, the birth of her children, rape, solitude, age. By Anton.

The unforgiving clay.

One floor above, the trundle of kittens down a hallway. Voices conjured by the fridge, the waterpipes, the night-settling of the old building.

Gleaned exclamations of love, or self-love, or the simple utterances of a woman living alone?

Pain or joy, or mundane punctuations into the telephone. The machine which he hates above all others.

But nowhere silence, even as darkness comes in.

He abandons the clay. He washes and dresses himself, and goes out on the street. The curtains are drawn, dull pink, in the windows above his studio. The air is tense with frost and exhaust fumes.

In the flat pool of a streetlight, maple leaves lie glued to the sidewalk. They look like the mud-tracks of gulls, beside the Duna.

He walks three blocks, down back streets, and waits for a streetcar. All the way downtown he stares at his own reflection past the people who face him. Yet he knows his stop; he steps down into the street and heads across, through the crawling traffic, to the blue neon gates.

It is early yet. Some of the men have dropped in on their way home from work. One has brought his own sandwiches in a brown paper bag. There are only two girls on the floor.

But it is still, for Tadeusz, the ante room to Hell.

The dreadful sounds pound from the overhead speakers – a fast, goose-step march with jiggling puppet-strokes stringing the beats together. It is all the same, and the spotlights flush on and off in the hues of hallucination while it plays. Not one heartbeat of stillness – the waitress cannot even hear you; it's a world that murders and outlaws language.

And they are so pretty, the children of the free world who parade in the spotlights, with the skin and the forms of angels, and the painted masks. Too young still to show the scars of this slaughter of innocence.

Who are their parents?

The men at this hour are middleaged like himself. Passive to flesh and lust, as if to TV. Voyeurs without the drive to prowl the back alleys in longing.

No sin. No joy.

Yet knowing this is here he's drawn once or twice a week, to the heart of the city, to watch.

He sees how the dancers, who cannot dance but just throw their limbs into the cage of sound, look down on the girl behind the bar as a lesser breed. And how she just smiles and serves them, and sees with her private eyes, saving up, perhaps, for her school fees.

He knows how *he* seems to her. The sullen regular in the corner, nursing his beer. A shadow-watcher who never smiles, or shows his eyes, or spends one penny on the dancers. He has imagined talking with her, in a coffee bar somewhere. If he were rich, he would leave her money, anonymously.

Two tables away, a girl sets down a stool, and steps out of her dress. The man with the brown paper bag has laid down five dollars. She arches, naked, back onto the table, her knee on the stool. Her hand brushes over her breasts, down her stomach, and caresses the inside of her outstretched thigh.

Tadeusz stares across at the private show. He watches the

slender hand on her thigh, lingers on the light pubic curls, the final taboo for his generation.

The girl swings around and kneels over the table. She mimes a hollywood pout and holds her young breasts just inches from the man's face. The man watches, impassive.

This is where Tadeusz stops watching the girls and focusses, with disgust and fascination, on the men.

She turns her back on her client. Kneels and bends over. Her hands reach back and spread her buttocks. Her fingers reach in to her vulva. The man watches, his hand feels its way into his brown paper bag and pulls out a sausage roll. It goes up to his face, and he chews, slowly, his blank gaze fixed on her anus and the flesh of her birth canal. Flakes of pastry cling to his lips.

Tadeusz sips at his beer. *Nazi*, he thinks to himself, *commissar, sloven.*

The waitress steps in front of Tadeusz. She points at his near-empty glass, mouths through the sound and light a question, contempt in her eyes.

He nods in shame. She stalks back to the bar.

V

Helena hears rumors the world is the work of angels.

At night as the radiator shunts and groans and carries messages on its flaking skin. From other numbered cells along the hall they murmur and moan, cry out and curse in their dreams. Or laugh, sometimes, like children surprised.

She lies in the darkness, below the judas window, and envisions the ateliers of Time and Space like the galleried levels within which she floats, suspended. The children of light, labouring on our Creation.

Cartoons, maquettes.

Thumb prints upon clay.

Forges and kilns.

Baroque elaborations, roccoco extravagance, romantic departures.

She ponders the Mongoose, the Mamba, the Garfish, the Paradise Bird. She considers the Mantis, the multiple Tapeworm cyst, the Karoo moths which cluster together and describe a perfect flower.

The angelic craftsmen extending endlessly the symmetrical blueprint, the two-eyed halves-made-whole, decreed for the animals.

Her fingers count out, on her belly, the ranks of Legumes. The Peas which extend from the manifold vetches to the towering timber-stack of the Brazil Tree.

The fourteen possible lattices in the crystals of lava.

Leucippus' grains of matter.

Time and Space removed from *then* and *now*, from the linear.

Are there recruits, to the angels? Do our dead sometimes aspire to make new connections?

Within this Creation, she senses other ateliers, and studios. The minds of artists, or Anton's beloved philosophers, maybe. Receptive minds, pregnable, fertile. In one sense, female.

Is this where the Sons of God lay down with the Daughters of Men?

She perceives that the world is a work of art. That works of art are sometimes the work of angels.

She is not sure at all that she wants to go home. She is not sure, at least, if she really wants to leave.

She reaches down, under her bed, to her locker. Feels through her clothes for the jar which Tadeusz brought for her. Her fingertips touch the cool porcelain flesh. The unadorned, almost translucent gift has become her icon for the workshop, the divine marriage chamber that his inarticulate mind must be.

VI

The nature of porcelain is a human miracle.

Its discovery was an act and conjunction of Providence.

It is clay combined with the matter that turns into clay – the dissolute, weathered flesh of earth's oldest rocks.

Porcelain is the stages of earth's decay, combined and reversed, passed into water and fire, and transformed into permanent harmony.

It is translucent. It sings when it is struck.

The clay is *Kaolin*, the rotting feldspar, *Petuntse*. It has been analysed, copied, perfectly (as a synthesiser "perfectly" copies Bach) reconstructed. But at some point in Time and Place, perhaps in the Hanyong Mountains, a potter discovered a saprolite pocket, where the clay and *petuntse* lay ready, combined.

The Chinese called it "White Jade"; the merchants of Europe tracked it down in laboratories.

At 2650 degrees fahrenheit, the *petuntse* vitrifies, while the *kaolin* holds the form which the potter created.

And of all the substances that a master-potter must learn, with all the provisos of accident, good and bad, porcelain is the most intractable.

It is the clay which does not forgive. Because it remembers.

It returns from the fire with every error and hesitation in its shaping exposed.

There are scientists who find a radiance in the infinite cells of Evolution which few of the faithful experience, facing Creation, who have come to believe that clay held the seeds of life. Clay had memory, therefore it recognised, therefore learnt, predicted, or guessed at least, therefore at length adapted. Life and intelligence came as one.

Adom, the red man, was formed out of clay, the dried alluvium of the Euphrates Valley.

Even the great workshops of the Orient used moulds for most of their porcelain.

Tadeusz throws the clay on his wheel.

Out of every twelve pots, he rejects eleven.

VII

Helena goes down to the showers in a line of twelve. The warders slam back the locks, throw open the doors and call each name. They step outside and fall into line.

They go single file to the end of the gallery. Two warders lead, one comes behind, clanging the cell-doors shut as she passes.

They wear grey housecoats, and black canvas slippers. Their towels are white, with a broad yellow stripe off-centre. It is the washbag in each right hand that is individual; and the shampoos inside, the conditioners, safety-razors, bright soaps.

At the foot of the steps they turn in to the shower section. The file breaks up. The guards stand in the vestibule and smoke.

They are the fourth group down this morning. The air is still dense with steam and perfume. The walls and the floor are wet, and warm.

"The end shower's fucked" a warder tells them "Don't touch it."

Helena lost her shyness long ago. Her heavy thighs, the flattening breasts on her broad chest are no more or less than the other bodies reveal, padding off through the steam. Scars of love and birth and age, of hate and of self-betrayal.

Some are crude and raucous, others keep to themselves.

But number 8 is a new girl.

They fall silent and watch as she hangs up her housecoat, the last. The warders look on, amused.

She lifts her chin and glares back at them. She is young, red-haired. She seems tiny before them. She has breasts that offer no clues – small, upright nipples which might have given suck or might always have been just so.

The steam gleams already upon her skin. It studs her pubic tuft with water-gems.

They snigger, but in the envy behind those sniggers is knowledge, and beneath that knowledge, so Helena believes, is love. In the unblemished skin they see the Fall, and they want that Fall because they know it will surely come, because their envies desire it, because their ugliness has no choice but to taunt. Because the Fall is the affirmation of innocence.

The girl is no innocent. Her eyes taunt back. She parades like a model between them, to the last of the showers.

"Hold it!" a guard snaps out. "You heard me – that shower's off limits." There is a towel hung over the faucet.

The girl's face is a mask against orders. She shrugs and steps towards another shower.

"There's electric current getting to it, somehow" another guard explains. "You could get fried."

The girl turns, stooping a little to conceal the slyness that brings her face to life. This is the real face surfacing – the person who has not dwelt in that flesh long enough to shape it.

She lunges for the last shower, and turns it on. She is screaming.

Do they all have this vision? Of electrical dancers, linked hand to hand, tugging against the current which runs through them, galvanised into death on the concrete floor?

As she flounders towards the shrieking girl, Helena wills herself through what may come, orders her body how to react when she loses control of it.

She is shrieking too, even as she reaches for the girl – she closes in, their screaming is a duet, indistinguishable. Despite her prevision, she hugs the girl instead of grabbing for her wrist. She hugs her against her belly and bears on through, charging into the sudden nausea of the current, her bladder voiding, her screams cut off, as they slam against the far wall and drop, tangled up with each other.

The water keeps falling upon the tiles. The women across the room are frozen, staring. The steam is like dry ice, on a stage.

The lights go out. The guards come in through the steam with their flashlights. It is mist in the forest, it is smoke in the streets. These are hunters, soldiers, searchlights.

The guards help them up, and lead them across to the doorway. The girl looks up into Helena's face: "Murdering cunt!" she says.

VIII

The echoes lie in ambush. Ghosts of the ghosts which only death can lay.

The woman is waiting in a car by the far curb. He senses her, something, as he turns in from the sidewalk, fumbling for his key. A shrinking around his ears, then sweat, prickling his shoulder blades.

When the car door slams across the street he stands rigid, on the step, key in hand. Waiting.

The door opens inwards at the same moment as her voice calls his name.

The woman from upstairs, a scarf on her head, is in front of him. Her smile of surprise is unnerved by his expression. The smell of the apartments escapes around her. Her eyes dart at the woman who comes up behind him.

"Excuse me" his neighbour murmurs, and steps around him. The other is right at his elbow: "Mr Dierrek?" His heart flinches. He turns slowly and stares in disbelief.

She is from the Parole Board: "Could we talk for a few minutes?"

"I just get in from work" he says.

The woman from upstairs adjusts her purse, lingering.

"It's about the hearing tomorrow. Helena, Mrs. Jemsky?"

"Helayna" he says. "I don't have to talk to you."

"It's in her best interests."

He hesitates. The woman from upstairs walks slowly away. "Okay, then" says Tadeusz. "What you want to know?"

Her face is accustomed to difficult clients, it adjusts itself. "I really have to come inside" she tells him. The veneer of civility.

"I'm supposed to see where – Mrs Jemsky would be living. If parole is approved."

The door's still ajar. She follows him in, down the hallway. He lets her in first. "Is the same place she lived in before" he says.

She looks around. "It's a nice apartment" she says "Bright. You keep it very clean." Tadeusz goes in the kitchen and sets his bag down on the counter. He takes off his coat and hangs it at the back door.

The woman unbuttons her coat as she walks round the living room. Her eyes go in at the open doorways. "What's in there?" she asks.

"Is private" he says. "My business, not yours."

"I am not the secret police, Mr Dierrek." She sits on the arm of the big chair.

"Sure you are" he says. "Will you take a drink?"

"Oh. Well, coffee maybe?"

"Coffee? Sure. You like vodka?"

"No thank you. Not on the job, anyway. Vodka's your drink?"

Tadeusz turns in the kitchen doorway and eyes her up and down. "Sure" he says "we like to drink, some nights a little, some nights a lot. Friday night we drink, we sing, we have good times there together." He eyes the couch, the rug in front of it, the chair on which she is sitting. He grins, savagely. She is very uncomfortable. "Sometimes we fight, also, too – just shout, okay?"

"Well" she begins "that's not the best –"

"Listen, lady" he says "don't tell me, okay? Helena can drink all she likes. She don't drive a car no more, ever, you know that, so that's that. You understand nothing."

"You're not helping" she says, to her knees. A brittle, rise-and-fall cadence, like a line from the movies.

"So how can I help?" He takes a bottle from the bag on the counter and pours a shot. "Drink?"

She forms a smile: "No thank you. The coffee?"

"Oh sure, I forget." He turns on the gas.

She crosses her legs in the silence. "It's not often I visit a home with no television." Bright again, professional.

"Is the enemy" he says.

"Yes, perhaps. Do you and Helena have much of a social group; friends?"

He sips at the vodka, sardonic. "We are okay. We read, we walk, I work, we are fine."

She looks round again. Her hand touches the bowl on the table beside her. "That's nice" she says. "Yes, it's a nice apartment.

"You see" she starts in again "we need to know what Helena is coming home to. She may not want to start work again, right away ..."

"Will she get this parole?"

"I can't tell you that" the woman says. "There's a good chance, though. She's done quite well."

"She will work" he says.

"There's a lot of stress, adjusting after prison, Mr Dierrek. You must try to understand."

"Lady" he says "I understand. I been in prison, Helena's husband live half his life in prison, die in prison, now she's in prison. I understand."

She has a small notebook out. "When were you in prison, Mr Dierrek? We weren't informed."

"Is that so?" he sneers. Then shrugs. "Long time ago, twenty years. In Slovakia."

"Oh I see" she says. "Well, that's different, of course."

"Is no different" he says. He empties his shot-glass. The kettle is filling the kitchen with steam. He turns off the gas, pours another drink. He leans at the doorway, watching her brown eyes.

"Now, you work as a janitor?"

He nods, slowly: "The Mercorp Building, on Wellesley."

"The thing is, you see, whether Mrs Jemsky and you can get by on your income ... "

"*Christ*, lady" he says. He puts down his drink and strides to the one closed door. He opens it, without turning a light on, and reaches inside. He comes back with an envelope: "Here, god damn it" and hands her a bank book.

"Okay?" he demands. "Helena can have what she needs from that. Okay?"

"My goodness" she says.

"So that makes the difference?"

"You didn't make this as a janitor."

"Not the secret police, huh? Everything is your business."

He leans on the couch back, glaring at her. He points – "In that room, I make pots, yeah? Pots. Are good pots. I am very good. Very expensive. I am not *mafia*, okay?"

"Pots" she says. "Oh. Well, I hardly thought you were *mafia*, Mr Dierrek!"

He goes back for his drink. "On the table, by you" he says, over his shoulder "Look. Pick it up. Look at it."

She does so. "You're very talented" she says. "It's very plain, but it's beautiful."

He comes round behind her: "Yes, beautiful." He leans over and flicks the bowl with his finger nail. It rings through the room, the note hangs.

"*D Sharp*" she says.

He laughs, she too. "You are in wrong job, maybe" he says, and his finger touches her arm, just inside the wrist, and traces the skin up softly to the pulse in her elbow. "If I could make porcelain that colour, Smokey, Caffée, Black."

"That's only skin deep, Mr Dierrek"

His hand tightens on her arm. "Turn around" he says quietly.

He holds her hand, with the bowl, up to the window. She can see her fingers, like x-ray shadows. "With porcelain" he tells her "you see through the skin."

IX

It was Anton's conviction that language, at heart, was national, specific and unexportable.

Stories, in their simplicity, could be told, and altered like folktales where they travelled.

Ideas, to a point, could be grafted to alien stock, since the evolution of language is the cumulative theft of ideas.

But though poetry was closer to mathematics and music than all other word-structures, it defied translation. You could never learn a new tongue well enough to understand things that illiterate natives would know. "The poets" he said "are not only sublime, but their wisdom stalks through the speech of their peasantry."

There were more reason's than Plato's for exiling the poets.

The room was packed whenever he gave that lecture. "Here

is a foreign religion" he started, brandishing volumes in turn of Goethe, Dante, Baudelaire, Whitman. "We can not be converted; we will never be true believers." A spare prose rendering of the liturgy was his prescription. That, and a knowledge of the language's sounds and cadences, might approach a communion.

Towards the end he would ridicule brilliantly Dante's beseiged malevolence, and then he'd break out in the passage that ends *Ben son, ben son, Béatrìcé,* so that tears came into his own, and the students' eyes.

As to their own language, he spoke of the Frenchman's *correspondances.* Correspondences everywhere which could become conjunctions. "But how" he'd conclude "how shall we ever know if we understand?"

Helena has tried to shake off the assault of misery. Tried to reduce to sadness the girl's vicious privacy.

She chose not to go to the library. She sits on her bed, hands folded between her thighs. The wing is silent. She has come back to the words.

She cannot grasp them in her own tongue, in any of the languages she speaks. They elude her with puns and subtexts, with echoes and imprecisions.

Just the words themselves, in her cell.

"Murdering cunt!" "Murdering cunt!" They become waves breaking in a cave. *Murdering cunt, murdering cunt, murdering cunt* ... It is not her language, the thing become the idea.

The scarred, white wall that faces her is the fabric of her mind. Upon it an image, suddenly playing. A vulva opening up to disgorge another vulva.

Like the fish in Breughel's "Proverbs".

Not the slit, the crease, the gash. This is the birth-mouth, wider than high, hinged like a shark's jaw, a frog's. Disgorging and swallowing like a lung, like the frog that can only swallow by pressing down on its meat with the blind prints of its eyeballs.

Mouths within mouths, a landscape of mounds that gape and swallow and disgorge each other to eternity.

Her daughter, somewhere, with a daughter perhaps.

Forward and back. Neanderthal, Pithecogyne, Eve.

This is how Tadeusz thinks, in images.

What Anton would not allow, though he understood it.

The luminosity of a child's nightmare.

Helena weeps silently. Her clasped hands swing from side to side. Her mouth is a stretched hole of pain.

The little girl, on the wet pavement beside the car, blood streaming with the dark rain out of her hair.

X

Tadeusz shakes out a clean sheet over the bed. He snaps it taut and it settles, almost perfectly placed. He moves slowly, methodically, from corner to corner, tucking the ends in, folding each side-flap over itself like an envelope. The hospital corners, army corners, the prison's.

The gauze curtains shift, from the draught in the window frame. There's a ragged margin of frost on the storm windows. The city is muffled by a late snow. Vapor plumes from the rooftops across the street, and all over Toronto, like smoke from the chimneys of Bratislava.

He unfolds a pillow slip, and catches its movement in the mirror on Helena's dressing table. He holds the pillow with his chin and eases the slip up around it. He sets it down at the bed-head and turns to regard himself in the mirror. He sits down at Helena's stool, and lays his hands flat on the walnut surface.

For all his vacuuming, and the weekly dust-and-polish, he still finds strands of hair, floated in from somewhere. Shreds of Helena – fine wavey filaments, dark blonde, kept long for his sake.

But her smell has departed. The powders and humble perfumes in her drawer smell of themselves – the alchemy they formed with her skin was vanished.

Only the green wool jacket in the closet, uncleaned, can summon her body still into this room. Sometimes he stands, half in the closet, with his face buried in its lining.

Sometimes he hears her voice in the other room. Calling his name, or singing. Never more than a word or two. When he is half-asleep, perhaps.

When his wheel whispers to a halt in the studio, he imagines he'll hear her moving, as the birds would be suddenly crying in the birch woods when the guns stopped firing.

He hears a siren, moving slowly two blocks away. A table scrapes overhead, a toilet flushes.

He opens the drawer, and feels past the bottles, under the handkerchiefs for the little box that he made her. He pulls it out.

He knows what is in it. She has told him, would have let him see, gladly; but it is her privacy. She would not take it, even, to the prison, for fear of defilement.

Yet he cannot stop himself, now. His hand trembles, and he senses that she, in her cell, must know what he's doing. Or at least she is thinking of the box.

Inside is a folded paper. Beneath that a lock of hair, flaxen, her daughter's. And a baby tooth.

He unfolds the paper, and sees Helena's writing. Within it, three brittle slips, cigarette papers. The faded pencil marks, his brother's words.

They are too faint to read. The folded sheet holds Helena's transcription.

The enlightened man, in the detachment of his irony, faced with the evils of war, oppression, arrest, is in effect a time-traveller.

The interest is less in how easily his poise and assumptions can be destroyed, but in the more abstract question: Are his values false, or simply relative or, in the end, literary?

He has one recourse only – Madness. He is Hamlet in the prison of Denmark, but is not in control: hence his disease is not feigned. But being released, by whatever means, Can he come back? Can his irony?

Tadeusz folds the papers back into the paper. He returns the box to its nest, and closes the drawer.

The words mean less to him than they had to Helena. Delivered one night by a man who had shared Anton's cell. She had turned away and read them at once, and had been filled, she said, with anger. What had this to do with her? She was enraged at the man who had locked himself out of her, becoming a monument more than a man. His cellmate had stayed, and in her grief and anger and her reaching for the one who had spent three years with this man's nakedness, she had made love to him that night on the couch, and again in her bed at dawn while the children watched from their bunks, stoical already, wakened by her cries.

Tadeusz leaves the bed unfinished, and goes out to his studio. There are tasks you can do when creation's unthinkable. The mechanical craft that refinishes or prepares. There are two pieces he's resolved to have done, if she gets the parole, if she comes home – when? – next week?

He turns on the radio. Knows the piece within two bars. It's a day of connections. Is it possible Helena is hearing this too? *The Sly Little Vixen*. He hums along with it, as he takes down the high-shouldered vase and begins to wipe a damp cloth across its skin. There's a burst of static on the radio, the wavelength buckles: the chatter of a taxi or ambulance despatcher, then Janacek again, drowned in the buzzsaw arpeggios of electric guitars and free-world male screaming...

Tadeusz hurls the vase against the wall, and reaches for another.

XI

"You were sent to prison *as* punishment, not *for* punishment."

Helena sits in the high-backed chair, facing the table. Her hands grip the seat, beside her thighs. She knows two of the four women here. One was at her last hearing too, unfriendly. There is no man, this time.

"Our job would be much easier if you had agreed to counselling."

The assistant warden leans sideways, to catch Helena's eye. She wears pearls over her jersey blouse, her eyes are concerned. "We've talked about this before, Helena. We offer professional help, and – well, Mrs Johnstone's quite right – how can we feel that you're helping yourself, when you won't co-operate?"

"Do I speak now?" asks Helena. Three heads nod. "I tell you before – I am not crazy."

"You certainly have a problem, Mrs Jemsky. Let's be brutally frank about this – you had two convictions for impaired driving before ..." Whether her voice tails off out of tact or for greater effect, it is hard to say.

It is hopeless. Helena shrugs. The assistant warden intercedes again. "Helena, this must seem like a trial to you, another trial, but it isn't. We are here to help you, to help you get on with your life. You have been a model prisoner, I have stressed that to the board. They also know about your very brave actions yesterday, in the shower room." Even Mrs Johnstone nods. Helena lowers her eyes.

"But you are very withdrawn. We need to know that you understand this punishment, that you will not – break out again into foolish behaviour."

Helena takes a long breath, and exhales. "What words do you want me to say?"

Mrs Johnstone's voice is tense with opinions: "We are not to be taken in by words, Mrs Jemsky. This not a charade."

"Helena" there's an appeal, complicit, in the assistant warden's grey eyes "we are looking for an excuse to let you go. Don't you understand?"

"No, I'm sorry – not an excuse, Miss Stasiuk, a *reason*. We need a very good reason, Mrs Jemsky, why we should offer you the freedom of the streets."

It is hopeless. Helena folds her hands in her lap. "What words do you want me to say?"

XII

"I used to watch you." Wherever these words occur in a story must be the pivot: the point at which the past moves into the future and is left behind.

Tadeusz has heard the words twice in his life, and will hear them at least twice more.

The stroke-tightened lips of his mother, beside the window: "I used to watch you, fighting on the lawn with Anton – already you were growing stronger than him. I feared so much for you both – I could not stop you fighting, but a woman alone fears to be sentimental. I remember you fighting over your father's green hunting-bag. Perhaps that was your last fight, I don't know." She was only two days from death. He lacked the heart to tell her that Anton had gone before.

And then in Vienna one of the camp guards, in exile himself. They sat in a bar near the station, and shared cigarettes. "I used to watch you take your walk outside in the snow. I came to expect you – you were the only one outside. I used to aim my machine-gun between your shoulder-blades and follow you with it around the yard." He laughed, and placed his hand on Tadeusz' forearm. "I knew then that if another prisoner didn't kill you, you'd get out alive."

But tonight it is Helena's voice on the phone.

"Tadeusz, I used to watch you leaving. I could not bear it. I could see you walking out through the gates and I thought in myself that I was killing you. I could not bear it. That's why I said no more visits. And I came to think that I did not want to be with you again, I thought that we should forget …

"Tadeusz, they have given me my parole. They want me to leave the prison, tomorrow. What should I do?"

Tadeusz can hear the woman on the pay-phone next to her. "What about *my* life? You fucking bastard, what about *me*?"

He leans his head on the kitchen doorway. "Helena" he says "I have had this phone in the apartment just to hear news from you. All I have got is wrong numbers, and people who try to sell me things. I am waiting for you – come home."

He replaces the phone, and then points a finger at it, like a child's make-believe pistol. He shoots it and shoots it and begins to laugh, quietly, crazily. He dances on one spot, in the living room. The world seems twice as big, all at once.

He rips the jack from its socket and goes out in the hallway. He will throw the phone into the street.

The woman from upstairs is checking her mail-box. "Here" he says, thrusting his hands at her "Here, lady – you want this phone? Is all paid for."

XIII

Tadeusz is released from sleep with such gentleness that he scarcely believes he was there.

The room is bright. It is still afternoon. He can feel Helena's eyes on his face. He reaches down for her hand before he can look at her.

She is barely smiling. She brings their hands up to her lips, and then to his cheek. The smell of her body breathes over him.

"I used to watch you" she says "in the garden on Tatry Street. You remember?" His eyes stay on hers. "Such a busy boy, in your own world there, in the corner under the terrace. Always on your hands and knees, for hours, while your brother was practising Chopin."

The gauze curtains rustle, the ceiling shivers with reflected sunlight. Tadeusz looks upwards, his left hand cradles his head on the pillow. "Yes" he says "the *Fantasie*, the *Etudes*, and me in the dirt by the apple tree.

"It was rich, that earth, black and sweet. There was Solomon's Seal and Lily of the Valley, a thousand snail shells – you could see the light through them, amber. That earth was old, but it wasn't exhausted.

"I collected china. Fragments of plates and bowls. I had hundreds of them, dug from the black earth. Not once did I find two pieces that fitted each other. I would make up the shapes, and the blue pictures, from the smallest evidence."

He smiles. "Now I think I was often right!"

"Are the houses still there?" she whispers.

"Yes" he says "of course. You remember the sunken lane, between our places, going down to the churchyard?"

"The cobblestones were red when it rained" says Helena "There were slate gutters to carry the water down.

"The ivy on the walls was full of honey-bees."

"Yes. I'd look down from my wall onto the heads of the pall-bearers, a few feet below. The bell would be tolling in the tower. I could read the names on the brass plates on the coffins."

He rolls over to face her. "And once" he says "I saw a girl looking over from the garden across that lane. She was blonde, and taller than me, and she was standing among the golden rods. I did not see her at first; she thought she was invisible.

"I thought she was beautiful. Her family had just moved in. I picked green apples from the ground by my feet – and pelted her with them!"

Helena stretches her legs, and relaxes them. Her laugh is a child's. "You missed" she says "Your face was red and your aim was terrible!"

His hand moves from hers and roves across her belly. He traces the blue-grey fissures in her skin, the marks of the children she has lost and which he never knew.

"I still feel invisible, sometimes" she says.

He takes her hand again. They lie looking up at the ceiling. The sounds of the city drift in, and are filtered out.

They have never been so close to each other, never so far apart.

For the moment each is almost entirely happy.

Acknowledgements

A line in the title story, "It is the beginning of loneliness", comes from Patrick Lane's poem, *Dominion Day Dance*. The theft was unintentional of course – writers do this: you absorb something so much into yourself that when it resurfaces it feels like your own vocabulary. Sometimes you catch yourself at it. It was too late in this case – the line was already essential to the story. Patrick Lane was sardonically unperturbed by my confession. And he's one of the bare handful of *makars* from whom it's an honor to borrow.

Brian Brett told me, one night in White Rock, about porcelain's memory.

Graham Howcroft told me, one night in St. John's, about glass's fluidity.

> Barry Callaghan took an axe
> And gave this manuscript forty whacks
> When I saw what he had done
> I gave it another forty one.

I am grateful for the time made free for me by a grant from the Canada Council.